Mornings

In

Two Pan

Two Pan: Book 1

B.K Froman

Morning West Publishing
Beavercreek Oregon

Morning West Publishing
Copyright 2014 Barb Froman

Scripture taken from the Holy Bible, NIV. Copyright 1973, 1978, 1984 International Bible Society, Used by permission of Zondervan Bible Publishers

ISBN:978-1938531-14-9

I believe that what we become depends on what our fathers teach us at odd moments when they aren't trying to teach us. We are formed by scraps of wisdom.

—Umberto Eco

To David, Greg, and Ken

"Use Time as a Tool, Not a Couch"

—John F. Kennedy

SOMETIMES THE DAYLIGHT in Two Pan, Oregon looks different than you'd expect. Every now and then it takes on a quality that you might say...has been "paused." Put on hold. Waiting for something to happen. The sun's rays seem to slow the minutes to a standstill or make an hour linger before moving on. Often, the sunsets glow with a sepia hue as though filtered through the fabric of some yesteryear.

You'll recognize this light when you see it. It has that same golden-drifting peculiarity that poured through school windows while you sat at your desk in the fifth grade, drawing ponies that could fly or cars that shot bolts of fire from their headlights. Meanwhile, at the front of the classroom, the teacher yammered about pronoun-antecedent agreement, and the hands on the clock didn't move.

Every now and then you'd look at her, mostly to be sure she wasn't sneaking up on you. You're smart like that. But cocooned in shafts of sunlight, you really couldn't see her standing on the shadowy side of the room. Instead, you studied the dust motes spinning in lazy loops. It made you look like you were watching the teacher. It also had the added benefit of making you seem interested in whatever she was jabbering about. This went a long way toward mitigating other infractions she might catch you doing when the clock didn't move. Like I said, you're smart.

Most folks on this dry side of the state are wise in that sort of way. The few residents still in Two Pan know about the daylight's tricks. Some say it's the Eagle Cap Mountains south of town, refracting the light. Others say it's the heat and haze of the day, trying to noodle its fingers into the canyons and arroyos only to be rolled back upon the squat-doodle little town by the cool breezes of twilight.

Whether it's physics, geography, or hoodoo which changes the light, the folks of Two Pan know better than to let it lull them into restful living. At this edge of civilization, there's always something growing up, falling down, caving in, breaking out, or passing by which should've been taken care of yesterday. It's what makes the people a little stubborn, a little creative, a little eccentric, and sometimes—a little sleepless.

If you think this is a bunch of foolishness—and don't believe that light changes time—just ask Jiggs Woolsey. At the moment you'll find him on the ground. He's sitting exactly where he tripped when he jumped backward. He's holding his breath, though he isn't aware of it.

Unmoving. Still as a rock with that wide-eyed stare you see on animals forever regretting their decision to cross the highway.

Time has paused.

The light shines off the broken white skull in the dirt in front of him. The snake coiled beside it gives its tail a rattle—a polite warning—reminding Jiggs that the light tricked him into this situation.

Common Sense Isn't Common

THE CROWS LIKED to get a head start on welcoming the dawn to eastern Oregon. Each morning, they gathered in the maple tree beside Jiggs Woolsey's bedroom and cawed their hellos, chittering plans for the morning. Jiggs reminded himself, as he did every day, to cut down the tree, even if it did shade his ranch house from the afternoon sun. The birds would have to fly half a mile to find another that size to host their breakfast meetings.

Awake. Dressed. He stepped out the door and onto his back porch, armed with an insulated mug of coffee for the ten-mile drive to Two Pan. To the east, a few ragged clouds held onto pinks and purples above a rising sun. Sky decorations. They wouldn't bring any rain.

A glance at the small house next door told him his Dad's truck was missing. Jiggs went back inside, hung up his hat and cracked four eggs into the frying pan that always stayed on the stovetop. If Ox Woolsey was at the Bar and Grill, Jiggs would eat at home.

He was smearing Lottie Lubach's pear jam on an over-cooked slice of toast when the creak of the backdoor reached the kitchen, followed by clomping on the mud mat.

"You don't need to stomp." Jiggs' voice carried tired frustration. "There's not enough dew in the county to muddy a toad, much less your boots."

"Well, if I stayed on cow paths and foot trails like you, that'd be true," Ox Woolsey said as he crossed the linoleum. Even at eighty-four, he still filled the kitchen, his white head turning to check the stove then the coffee. He sat down at the same spot he'd occupied when he'd lived in the house. Head of the table, nearest the door, legs angled into the room.

Jiggs glanced at him and stabbed a knife into the butter. He kept it in the covered butter bowl his wife and his mother had used, so it was room temperature and spreadable, but it wasn't smoothing over the top of the jam. Things often got out of order when his dad was around.

Ox picked up the butter knife as soon as Jiggs laid it down. He nabbed the other slice of toast leaning against his son's plate. "Fired this one a little too hot," he said, knocking the black edges off.

"I like it that way."

"Sure you do. Pass the jelly."

With the back of his hand, Jiggs nudged the half-pint jar toward his father and kept eating.

"You make more than one cup of that stuff you call coffee?"

Jiggs didn't answer.

When Ox returned to the table he had scraped the remaining eggs from the skillet onto a plate, added a new piece of toast, and carried a mug of steaming coffee cradled in a salad saucer. Pulling his chair up to the table for serious business, he poured the coffee in the saucer and added milk as though preparing the dish for a cat. "I been up to Blank Map this morning," he said around the eggs he forked into his mouth. "Only counted twenty head. You need to get in that downslope thicket and see if the rest are there."

"That's where they were yesterday."

4

Before the old man could snort a comment, a sleepy voice mumbled, "Morning, Gramps. What's today's complaint?" Nap had entered the kitchen, still in baggy pajama pants, one eye closed as he scrubbed his hand through his hair. The bare-chested twenty-three-year-old had reached the full six-feet of his father and grandfather's height. Jiggs glanced between his old man, who was missing the bottom of his left ear, and his son, who still had all of his body parts and the lean muscle young men carry before they're exposed to years of ranching, too much beer, and pie with ice cream.

"Morning, Sleeping Beauty. Got a job for ya." Ox took a big bite of toast. "We're gonna start rustling cows from your dad." The old man shook his head as though he'd have to go as far as a big city to find such stupidity. "We'll have the meat at Grubbs or on somebody's barbecue grill before he even knows they're missing. Already been up north. Couldn't find three—"

"How many times did you drive off the road?" Jiggs piled his remaining scrambled eggs onto his toast, mashing them into the jam so they'd stick. He didn't look at the old man. He didn't need to. He could feel the glare searing the side of his face. It was a dirty trick to pick on the old guy's driving, but he'd developed it as a lifeline after forty-five years of shouldering criticism. Jiggs stood and carried his egg sandwich to the door. "Hope you at least ran over some gophers on your morning blitz." He paused long enough to look at Nap. "Your grandpa ate your breakfast. I'm fixing fence posts on Starvation Creek this morning." He turned and left.

"You leaving these dishes for somebody else to clean up?" Ox's voice had that get-back-here threat to it.

Jiggs kept walking. "You live next door. Remember?" Behind him Ox's voice rumbled, "Leave that plate right there, dammit. It'll be waiting for him when he gets back."

Two steps into the yard, Jiggs heard breaking ceramics and flatware clattering across the floor. Dropping his egg sandwich, he wheeled on his boot heel and hurried back to the kitchen.

Nap kneeled on the floor picking up the pieces of Jiggs' plate. Ox sat in his vinyl-padded chair, his teeth clenched, his mouth pulled in a straight line. He slowly pushed away from the table and stood. No one spoke as he passed through the door, leaving a feeling of burnt air floating through the kitchen.

Jiggs picked up the knife that had somersaulted against the cabinet, spackling pear jam onto the door.

Head down, Nap's cowlick and bedhead made his short, brown hair peacock-up in back. The young man's words were surly and sharp. "I've got this."

Jiggs abandoned him to floor duty and carried Ox's plate to the sink. "You want these eggs? He didn't finish them."

"What I want..." Nap looked at his father, his forehead furrowed with the pained look of a man backed into a corner and forced to fight. "I'm tired of being caught in the crossfire. Gramps didn't mean to make me drop the plate. I ignored him. Cleared the table anyway. He grabbed my arm. I dropped the plate. End of story."

Jiggs tossed him the dish sponge to wipe the floor. "I miss your grandmother. She could keep him in line."

Nap gave his dad a meaningful look. "And mom kept you in line." He continued wiping the floor as silence bled into the room. After a moment, the sponge flew to the sink with more force than necessary. He stood and dumped the pieces of ceramic in the trash. The jangling sound of the shattered plate broke the quietness.

Jiggs let out a sigh. "This is what happens when three hard-headed men live together."

"Then I'll gladly go back to college. When my roommates got out of line we took it outside and knocked some common sense into each other. I can't do that to you or Gramps. I need to move out. Find my own place."

"I hope not." Jiggs gave his son a half-smile, shaking his head. "Without you around, I'm afraid your granddad and I might throttle each other. And secondly, common sense isn't as common as you think. C'mon, I'll take you for breakfast. I dropped mine in the dirt, hurrying back inside."

Nap shook his head, gazing at the floor. "I'll fix a bowl of cereal."

Jiggs replayed their breakfast as he lugged rocks. A mindless task. The last time he'd done this, he'd been Nap's age, helping Ox reinforce the corner posts of the fence.

"The land hates man-made additions," Ox had told him. "The earth's skin cracks in the summer and puckers in the winter, trying to push out these posts like they're pimples."

It had proven true. They'd piled a pyramid of stones at each corner of the property. Then every twenty feet down the fence line, they'd built more rockjack anchors to keep the posts upright. Even so, years later some of them leaned, leaving slack in the wires, letting cattle push through the fence.

Taking his hat off, Jiggs wiped his forehead. It was long past noon. Breakfast had played out hours ago. He rested a foot on the shovel he used to pry up rocks. His breaks were becoming longer than his rock-lugging time. Letting the shovel fall over, he tromped across the pasture toward the small creek along the back side of the property. This time of year, the snowmelt would numb his fingers and make his eye sockets cold when he splashed the clear water on his face. It would be enough to keep him going to finish the last two rockjacks.

Ash and small cottonwoods had grown along the creek. Their budding leaves, no bigger than squirrels' ears, made lacy patterns on the streambed. The dry streambed.

Jiggs looked right and left. Small, round rocks dotted the sandy bottom. He kicked several out of place. The pockets they left in the sand weren't even damp. The water had been running last fall. He'd fixed the fence along the creek to keep the cows from mucking up the entire stream.

He walked the distance to the wide spot where homesteaders had dug out the channel to create a pool. Their old house was gone, but evidence of their lives remained. Ditches and rotting wooden gates cut through the land where they'd diverted the flow to irrigate. He checked the earthen dams to make sure water hadn't broken through. Everything was dry.

At one time, the dip pool had been good size, but now dead weeds and grass choked the edges. In the moving shade and light under the trees, the sandy bottom glittered with promises. But then, all the creeks in the county were flecked with bits of shine: mica, quartz, and even specks of gold the size of a bug's eye. A row of flat stones lay in the middle of the stream like a long six-foot pile of books. He'd never seen it before, but the flowing water would have covered it. It reminded Jiggs of the old miners' claims he'd seen around washouts.

Stepping over the weeds, he squatted to inspect a white rock doming through the sand. Pure white quartz, the companion of gold, was never this size in the valley. Surely it was a trick of the light.

He scratched the grit away, finding a layer of compacted pebbles. The dome was larger than he'd thought. He stood and kicked around it with the heel of his boot. The hard swing of his foot made him stumble, scattering flat rocks as he stepped through the pile.

A brown stick beside his boot kinked into an S-shape.

He jumped back. Bone crunched as he fell. The heel of his boot prised a white skull from the ground, flipping it into the air. As it landed in front of him, the rattlesnake struck it.

Jiggs froze. So did time.

Good Judgment Comes From Experience

JUST EASE YOUR gun out real slow, slower than sunrise. Then shoot it. Jiggs could hear his father's voice rolling through his mind. *Oh? You don't carry a gun? Guess you're gonna die, Son.* It was a useless message, but after forty-five years, his dad's voice was stuck in his head. Even if his old man were here, he wouldn't do anything. He'd stand back and let Jiggs contemplate the predicament he'd gotten himself into.

"This isn't the wild west anymore," Jiggs mumbled loud enough to make the snake, three feet from his boot, maraca-shake his rattles.

Ox was the only person he knew who carried a gun into the pasture. It had been handy in a couple of situations, but the other nine thousand ninety-nine times it had been in the way. Jiggs followed Hop Hopkins' example when it came to guns. Every summer, the old rancher had hired a team of "young bucks" to do his heavy lifting. The morning they were cutting lodge pole pines for fence posts, one of the teens found a rattler moving slowly in the chill of the shadows. Sol Meyers forked the reptile to the ground with a stick.

"Give you five bucks if you can fling him to that big boulder downhill." Jiggs had grinned at Sol. "Grab him by the tail. He can't bite upside down."

"Bull shit." Sol kept pressure on the stick as the snake's body coiled. "They can move any which way to fang you. Even through water. Don't even have to cock to strike."

"I heard you can wear 'em down," Dooley Monroe said. "Make 'em keep striking 'til they can't raise their head anymore." The three of them bent from the waist, inspecting the snake.

Sol looked at the others, a grin spreading across his mouth. "Well, let's just see. Get ready to move, girls." He lifted the stick. Yelling and cussing followed as the boys ran.

The rattler's tongue flicked the air several times.

"Leave it be. It'll slither off." Jiggs backed farther away, amazed how a few steps allowed the brown reptile to blend into the dirt and weeds.

"I'm not working out here..." Dooley's voice pitched higher, "knowing I could accidentally step on the log that sucker is hiding under. Besides, you know it has a buddy around."

"Here, watch this." Sol pulled a long branch from their limb pile and poked at the snake. It rattled its tail and opened its mouth, showing a milky-white lining. Sol circled one way then the other. At the third jab of the branch, the rattler lunged. It was piston-fast, rising, striking, dipping, and then rising and striking again.

"Shit!" Sol dropped the limb and jumped back. "Did you see that?" he yelled, but it was lost in the midst of "Whoooooooa!" and the whoops young men make when they're playing with something that could kill them.

"See if he can strike again," Jiggs shouted. Something hit him on the back of the head. He saw stars. He blinked, staring at his straw hat that now lay on the ground.

Hop Hopkins strode by. "Shut up. I don't have time to run you ladies to the morgue today."

At six foot four, he was what folks called, "a big ol' boy," and they didn't mean fat. His fifty-four-year-old body walked with a slight forward tilt, favoring the right knee. He complained every bone and joint ached because they'd all been busted at least once from breaking broncs. He walked behind Sol, who was teasing the snake again, and smacked him on the back of the head. The boy's hat flew off. The snake bit it as it landed.

"What the hell?" Sol scowled and rubbed his nape.

"Dooley! C'mere." Hop pointed at the boy then indicated a spot beside Sol.

"I didn't do nuthin'," Dooley whined as he cut a wide arc around the snake.

"Exactly. You're not solvin' the problem. You're not workin'. You're doin' *nothin'*." Hop knocked the branch from Sol's hand, mumbling, "Good grief. You're all like a buncha pups." He looked at Jiggs. "Get my gun outta the truck."

Still rubbing his head, Jiggs jogged twenty yards to where the truck was parked. When he returned with the .22 rifle, Dooley was rubbing the back of his head and looking hangdog. Jiggs felt a surge of respect for their boss. Unlike his dad, Hop handed out justice for all.

"Now tell me, you morons. Why can't I wet down a tree without you three having a tea party with a snake?" Hop sighted down the barrel.

"We were seeing if it could strike if we tired it out," Sol said.

Hop lowered the gun and looked at the sixteen-year-old. He waited a moment then asked softly, "Well, whadja learn?" Sol, the broad-shouldered quarterback of the junior varsity team, seemed to shrink to sixth-grade size. His shoulders jacked up and down in a quick shrug. Hop looked around. "Any of you Einsteins discover anything?"

He gave a disbelieving headshake at their silence. "Boy howdy." He jammed the gun into Jiggs' hands as he walked away.

The boys looked at each other. "You want *me* to shoot it, sir?" Jiggs knew he could hit it. Probably. Well...maybe not on the first try with everybody watching him.

"No," Hop said as he walked past him again, carrying one of the axes they'd been using to limb trees. He took two quick, long steps as he swung downward. The blade planted in the ground behind the reptile's head. The tail gave a rattle. The body slowly twisted, its belly turning toward the sky. "What I want—is for you boys to learn to finish a job once you start it. Don't piss around." He yanked the axe from the ground, turned, and walked away.

Jiggs stepped forward to get a closer look at the rattler in its death twist. Sol was pointing to his chest and mouthing, "*Dibbs*" on the rattles.

"Good judgment comes from experience," Hop called without looking back. "Unfortunately, experience usually comes from bad judgment. So leave the damn snake alone. You got work over here. Put the gun back in the truck, Jiggs."

The boys reluctantly returned to the pile of tree boles. Jiggs said, "Dad always keeps a gun handy when we're out working."

"This isn't the Wild West anymore, though Ox probably thinks so. Course...maybe you can't blame him."

"What d'you mean?" Jiggs asked.

Hop stared at him a moment then pulled his leather gloves from his belt. "You know, life is hard on an old fart like me. I have to do all the heavy work while my summer peahens cluck and dance around a snake. Now put the gun away and get back here."

Dooley watched Jiggs walk down the road. "What if there's another one, Mr. Hopkins?"

"You've got an axe, don't you?" He flexed his bicep. "Put some muscle on your little chicken wing and swing it like I just showed you."

A slow rattle brought Jiggs back to the moment and his latest snake. He didn't have an axe. He didn't even have his shovel, which he'd used all morning for this very reason. He knew better than to put his fingers under a rock. He might find a snake hanging off his knuckles. If Ox heard about this, he'd bring it up every day. Probably have it published in the paper.

It felt like he'd been sitting there an hour. The sunlight outlined the arrowhead shape of the reptile's brown and black scales, making them appear like shiny rows of armor plating. The rattling had stopped. The S-shape behind the triangular head still hovered in the air. A red tongue flicked at him, tasting the scent of his adrenalin and sweat. It looked to be a four-footer. If it were true that it could only strike half of its body length, he should be safe.

And even if he were bitten, he'd probably have time to drive himself to a hospital—if he were only bitten once. And if there wasn't much venom. He'd learned a few things since he was sixteen, thanks to that outdoor guy on TV who went into the wild with nothing but a flat bicycle tire and a Snickers bar. Rattlers often didn't inject venom on objects too big to eat. Jiggs straightened his spine and sat taller.

His focus dropped to the skull. It lay on its side, the temple caved in where his heel had crushed it. Some museum expert would have something to say about that. He felt bad about putting his foot through someone's head.

It had to have been there a long time. There wasn't any hair or cloth around it. No tribe would put a body in a streambed. Only white men did that. He'd heard the early settlers had hanged horse thieves from the cottonwoods, the tallest trees in the area, and then buried them in the sand—easy digging.

Without moving his head, he glanced upward. These trees were too small for rope parties. Everybody in the area looked for cottonwoods. "Trees of life" they called them because they only grew near water. Leave it to the pioneers to decorate them with death. He came from a strange bunch of people. Maybe the skull was one of the early Woolseys.

He moved slightly, trying to settle away from the rock poking him in the backside. The snake gave a slow *tick-tick-tick*, a metronome counting off the sluggish time.

"Bound to happen," he muttered. This was the limit. His morning had begun with an argument, now he was sitting in the dirt, talking to a snake like it was a party. And this time a skull had been invited to the shindig. Quietly, he told the snake, "As Hop Hopkins would say... 'It's time to finish what I started.'"

The rattles clicked a little faster. Jiggs tensed his legs, took a deep breath, and heaved. Sand and pebbles flew forward. He moved backward. The snake lunged. The pink-white insides of its mouth bloomed and widened. Fangs struck the sole of his boot. Jiggs scrabbled on palms and heels. In the flying sand, he lost sight of the snake. For all he knew it could be snapping like a crocodile or racing up his pant leg.

As soon as he felt the weeds under his hands, he pushed to his feet and ran twenty feet into the pasture. When he stopped, he stomped, doing a little jig, though he wasn't sure why, then he patted his legs and inspected his body. There was a mark on the bottom of his boot, but no puncture holes.

In fifteen minutes he returned to the dry pond with the shovel. The tree shadows had moved eastward as though time had finally shaken loose. The snake had slithered away, which was fine. Jiggs figured they'd both won the standoff. No need for killing.

He left the skull where it lay. It seemed wrong—and creepy—to put it beside him on his pickup seat and give it a ride to his house. Tomorrow he'd tell Sol Meyers, who was now sheriff. And Sol would surely ask what his dad knew about the skull. After all, the land had been in their family for five generations.

Jiggs silently groaned. Heaviness weighted his gut. It climbed his throat, tasting like ash. His shoulders tightened as he walked back to finish the rockjacks. He'd gotten past the snake, now he had to talk with his father about a skull. He'd almost rather deal with the snake again.

Forgive Your Enemies

THE FORD F-150 rattled down the long gravel driveway to the big one-story house with a front entryway that no one used.

Katie Woolsey, Jiggs' wife, used to keep a pot of flowers on the steps. Before that, Lisette Woolsey, Ox's wife, had kept the cat's bed next to the door. After both of them had passed, the wind did the courtesy of blowing away the flowers and the tattered mat, painful reminders of a livelier household. Now a family of spiders rented the eaves, displaying their weaving techniques from the thick craftsman-style support posts. Leaves and dirt met in the corners by the disused door. Anyone who was trying to get rid of gossip or zucchinis came through the side entrance of the mud room.

Ox Woolsey stood thirty yards away in front of his small house, staring to the west. He'd built the little cottage fifty years ago for his dad, so that he, Lisette, and their boys didn't have to put up with the spineless drunk. Now it was his home. He'd moved from the big house when Jiggs had a family. He hadn't complained. That was the way of getting damnable old.

A truck door slammed. He turned as far as his stiff shoulders allowed. It wasn't enough. Used to be, he could hear a vehicle coming a mile down the road. Either the damn cars were running quieter or the road had eaten most of its gravel.

He'd have to get onto the county commissioners to part with a little money to grade and rock their road again.

Putting a hand on the wood rail where they tied horses, he steadied himself as he took a half step back and twisted to see who'd driven in. He and Jiggs locked eyes for a moment. Neither acknowledged the other. Their silence carried unspoken words best left to the past. He turned away and removed his hand from the railing, irked that he'd been caught contemplating the sunset like an old man on a bench. The underbelly of the sky was ribbed with orange clouds. The honey-glow of evening crept in from the north and south.

It was a hell of a note when the only son he had left wouldn't call out a hello. Even strangers riding by a forest camp shouted a "Hey there." But Jiggs had too much of chip on his shoulder to respect old ways. He'd always been a jackrabbit. Coddled when Lisette was alive, he jumped from one project to another, doing a half-ass job on all of them. Pax had been the easy-going one, the one with enough sense to follow instructions.

Ox consciously ignored Jiggs' nearby busywork. He stared at the field, the black cattle, and this year's new models romping near their mothers. An old black and white Holstein milk cow, ran after them, then stopped and began chasing her own tail. He heard Jiggs throw a hose at the base of the old lilac bush and turn on the faucet.

"What're you staring at, Dad?"

Ox took no notice, feeling it was too late to gab now. Any civilized yahoo would've started with conversation when he got out of the truck. It didn't matter. His son would repeat himself, a little louder, a little annoyed. Served him right.

"Everything all right?" Jiggs stood next to him, squinting across rolling pasture land.

The boy had grown taller than him. Ox straightened his spine. It made his hip hurt. He relaxed back into his eighty-four-year-old, slump-shouldered curve, wishing they could have a civil conversation without his heart popping flip-flops in his chest. It would all be easier if his son could grasp hold of what was most important.

Jiggs' little wife had been good at getting them to converse. Katie would bring up her family's potato farming business in Idaho. She'd throw in facts about pottery making, turkey vultures, and interesting whatnots. He and Jiggs both knew what she was doing, but they played along and talked decently. When they didn't, she'd say, "Don't make me get the flyswatter, because you know I'll do it."

The house hadn't been the same since the cancer took her. He smoothed his hand over his white hair as though rubbing memories from his mind. It seemed they'd all gotten a little bit lonelier each of the fifteen years that had passed. Or maybe it was just him. The rest of them had gotten more hard-headed.

"Do you see smoke? Do we need to check on something?" Jiggs asked louder, scanning the horizon.

Ox let out a huffed breath. "Can't I watch Harriet without being pecked to death?"

"That old milkbag has dementia. I never know if she's gonna butt me or lick me when I go out there." Jiggs watched the black and white Holstein hop around like a bee was chasing her. "Why don't you send her to the dog food factory?"

"Because she's earned the right to grow old, and I like having a quirky cow. No matter how dark things get, she makes me laugh, dammit."

Jiggs turned away. "Sorry." He sprayed a few other plants then turned off the water. He threw the hose aside, then glanced at his father and began coiling it instead. "You got dinner plans?"

"Bologna."

"I'm burning a hamburger. You want one?"

Ox looked at him. "Nap won't be here. He went to a movie in Joseph." He could see Jiggs understood what he was saying. There'd be no one to take the sharp edges off their barbs. No one to referee.

"You prefer hamburger or steak? Freezer's full." Jiggs used the side of his foot to shove the coiled hose next to the foundation then put his hands on his hips, meeting Ox's gaze.

"You know what I'd really like? A good ol' pot roast." He held up his hand before Jiggs could speak. "I know we don't have time to thaw one, much less figure out how to barbecue it, but darned if I don't miss your mother's pot roast." He shook his head, staring at the lilac bush. "Katie was a good little cook, too. She could turn out a..." his words faded. Both men watched the water drip off the green leaves where Jiggs had splashed it. "Lisette loved it when the lilacs bloomed."

"Yep."

Ox took a step away. He was standing too close. Jiggs moved too. Ox kept walking, both men departing without a word, heading to their houses. His door groaned about being opened. Across the gravel drive Jiggs shouted, "Hey!" Ox felt charitable. No need to pretend he hadn't heard. He turned to see Jiggs leaning out the doorway of the big house.

"Burgers will be ready in twenty minutes if you want one. We should have Nap figure out how to cook a roast." His son grinned at him. "He's one of those progressive college men who can learn it all from his phone."

Ox gave him a half-smile and a single wave of his hand. "Sounds like a project." He closed the door, his smile reaching his eyes. Maybe he would have a decent conversation with the boy before one of them died.

"I fixed the rockjacks on Starvation Ridge this morning." Jiggs slid a thick burger dripping with juice onto the plate on the patio table.

"You didn't see to the cattle at Blank Map like I told you?" Ox asked.

"Nope."

"Well, that's just great." He gave the ketchup bottle four hard squeezes, blanketing the patty in red sauce.

"Nap checked. Stop your worrying."

"I built this place by worryin'. You must think cattle grow on trees, because—"

"No. Money grows on trees." Jiggs sat down across from his dad and shook potato chips from the bag onto his plate. "The stork drops off the baby cows."

"Always with jokes."

"Yep."

In silence, the men built their burgers, piling slices of purple onion and cheese onto buns. Ox stuffed a Cheeto into the edge of his burger. Each time he took a bite, he wedged another cheesy-fried puff between bun and meat. Jiggs went to the fridge and returned, holding up two beers. Ox gave a nod. Jiggs slid an Oly in front of him.

"Do you know any reason why the creek would stop running at Starvation Ridge?" The bottle hissed as Jiggs sat and twisted the cap.

Ox stared, the burger half-way to his mouth. "The hell you say?"

"It's completely dried up. I walked up to that old homestead and—what's the matter?"

Ox had dropped his burger, making Cheetos bounce off his plate. "It went dry once before, back in the '50s."

"Drought?"

"Nope." Ox slowly shook his head and picked up his burger again. "Cal Mosley, a weasely son of a bitch. I'm not kidding, he had a skinny, little body, no shoulders, and a pinched face. You'd swear he was sired by a rat. He had a bunged-up foot which kept him from hard work. He got the bright idea to pull what little gold there was out of the stream. 'Course, he was too lazy to work a rocker or sluices, so he tried to run it through channels so the flecks settled out on the turns. It looked like an acre of Chinese water puzzles."

"I thought those were irrigation ditches," Jiggs said.

"That's what the little shit claimed. But he'd have to plant something to irrigate it, wouldn't he? All he could grow was stupider. He cut the water off from me and another rancher downstream."

"How'd you get it back?"

"This is what I'm talking about. Somebody somewhere is always plotting to take what's yours. You've gotta protect your family and property. How would you go about gettin' it back?"

"I'd talk to him."

"George Jugenmeir and I tried that. We went up there to see where the water had gone. The little weasel stumbled out of his hovel, shooting his .410. I don't know if he shot over our heads on purpose or missed because he was drunk. He was a mean little bastard."

"You didn't shoot back?" Jiggs said flatly. "I thought that's why you carried a gun."

Ox squinted at his son the way a woman looked at a dog that had crapped at her front door. "I can't tell if you're bein' funny or mouthy. Either way, you sound stupid. We sicced the sheriff, Topeka Butler, on Mosley. The county was payin' him, not us, to take bird shot."

"So the sheriff was really the one who got the water flowing again, not you."

"No. Topeka hated Mosley because he caused a world of trouble, but Top was a lazy-ass sheriff. He liked to wear the badge, drive the cruiser, and that was about it. Whenever he was forced to arrest the little rat for being drunk and bein' a public nuisance, Top would cuff him to the door handle and make him walk alongside the cruiser. If he put him in the back,

Cal would puke in the patrol car for spite. Top visited the place several times. Mosley finally took off. Probably realized running moonshine paid better than the spitwad of gold in that creek. I ended up buying the land to keep it from happening again."

"But it's dried up again. You're saying someone's mining? Higher up on the ridge?"

Ox looked at his watch. "We'll get the flashlights and go over after dinner."

"Eat your burger. We can't see anything tonight. I'll look in the morning."

"You couldn't track a dog through wet cement. You don't get it. It's happening again. Somebody is divertin' the stream." He nailed Jiggs with a glare. "One day you'll learn too late that nobody's going to take care of things for you. People will take it from you. Forgive your enemies, but don't forget their names. I don't know why you insist on being the slowest brain on this ranch. And that's saying something when you think how dimwitted cows are."

"Well, maybe you can educate me about the skull I found in the streambed."

Ox stared at his half-eaten burger a moment.

"Did you hear me? I found a skull."

"What?" Ox squinted and waved him away like he was a fly pestering his thoughts. "Well...they all get dull."

"What gets dull?"

Ox pushed back his chair, looked at his watch and stood. "Just sharpen it. You still know how to use a whetstone, don't you?"

"What?" Jiggs squinted. His voice notched up another decibel. "I didn't say something was dull. I said skull." He rapped his knuckles against his head, speaking louder, "Skull!"

"Oh hell." Ox waved his words away again. "The whole countryside is littered with empty heads and bones. Bury it and let it rest."

"Human?" Jiggs squinted. "You're telling me that in the middle of the property we've owned for most of five generations, there's a skull, and it doesn't bother you?"

"No. It don't. And if you were any kind of rancher, you'd be more concerned about getting water to those cattle tonight." Ox moved toward the door, carrying his hamburger.

"I cut the fence," Jiggs said as he stood up. "They can get to a feeder spring coming off the side of the hill. The herd is fine for now. Finish your supper. You don't need to be tromping over rocky hillsides in the dark. I ran into a rattler there today."

"Snakes don't bother me. I carry a pistol," Ox stepped out the kitchen door into the mudroom.

"Suit yourself. I'm turning it into Sol in the morning."

"No..." Ox stepped back through the door. His face hardened into the look of a man who liked to hamstring the feebled. "You're not."

Jiggs widened his stance, bracing for the smack that was sure to follow. "I am." He stared at Ox. "Why wouldn't I?"

"Damn it!" Ox's fist came down on the counter. The hinged lid of the bread box fell open, banging the cabinet top. A box of dishwashing powder fell over, white granules spilling across the Formica, peppering onto the floor. "You call somebody, and the state will have that field taped off for months, plowing up the grass from here to Ontario. We won't be able to use it all summer 'cause they'll be lookin' for historical junk. The road will be full of rubberneckers kicking up dirt, driving by to see what's happening. Somebody will wander out from some historical society and need the fence cut in five places before they figure out what they want. All this because some pissant decided to die there and not fifty feet to the north on BLM land. Our cattle won't be able to graze. They won't make weight by market time. The fence will have to be fixed and grass replant-ed. And you know who'll be left holdin' the bill for all that useless snooping? Me!"

"You don't know—"

"No, dammit." Ox pointed his finger, inches from Jiggs' face. "It's you who don't know."

Jiggs wore the smoldering stare of a man who'd stopped listening. His fists clenched at his sides.

"Shi-it," Ox rubbed his hand over his forehead. "All this over what's probably the head of a coyote."

"I know the difference. I put my foot through somebody's temple."

"Bub, there are times you wouldn't know if you were step-pin' on your own head. You never were reasonable. Pax was the one I could talk to." Ox turned and stomped through the doorway, his voice weighted with regret and exhaustion. "I'll look at it in the morning. In the meantime, just shut up."

It's Hard to Put a Foot in a Closed Mouth

THE NEXT MORNING Jiggs peeked out the window and told the squawking crows he would cut down their tree someday. Ox's faded-blue Chevy was gone. If his dad had left last night, Jiggs would've heard the engine turn over. He'd awakened at 1:45, as he did most nights, listening for the phone to ring. Sleep had eventually crept back over him as he waited for a call that would never come.

It was more likely Ox had taken off around five when the sky had lightened to gray. For all Jiggs knew, his dad was already lying on Starvation Ridge with his leg busted or his head cracked open. He wasn't as steady on his feet as he used to be—though he'd cuss anyone who mentioned it. A climb up the side of the ridge was necessary before seeing the sheriff. Once again, Ox had fouled up plans for the day. Jiggs let out a long breath.

Last night had been a bungled mess. He thought he knew what to expect after forty-five years of listening to Ox heap damnation on the government, environmental organizations, and anyone who came on his property unannounced and uninvited—which included door-knocking missionaries. Each March, between calving duties, they made a mad dash to their tax man. Jiggs was relieved they could never stay long. Ox loudly cursed every penny he owed in taxes, making Jiggs wish he could crawl under his chair in the accountant's office and pretend they weren't related. Thank the Lord the taxes were in and calving season was over. The topsoil between him and his dad had worn thin years ago. They'd become boulders scraping against each other, waiting for the earthquake that would split them loose.

"Morning," Nap said as he entered the kitchen and opened the fridge. "We outta milk?"

"You drank the last of it, so you need to get a gallon."

"I left a little so I wouldn't be last."

"Sheesh. A halfa teaspoon. Where'd you learn to get out of work like that? You want eggs?"

Nap nodded. "I got ed-u-cated. Got me a college de-gree." He thumped his chest. "I learned a little animal husbandry and a lot about finding loopholes in the system. Where's Gramps?"

"Probably checking the work I did yesterday. I found a—" He watched Nap bounce hot toast on his fingertips and pull a plate from the cabinet at the same time.

"Whad'ja find?"

Jiggs hesitated a moment before saying, "Nothing."

"I'm the mushroom around here." Nap slapped an opened jar on the side a couple of times, making grape jelly glop onto his toast. "You keep me in the dark and feed me bullshit. Nobody tells me anything."

"Yesterday, I told Ox that you checked the Blank Map herd. Do it today. I don't want him trying to round up those cows."

"He won't find the chips in their ears. When are you going to tell him we've chipped them like city-folk's dogs and all their information is on computer?" Nap asked.

"Five years after he's dead should be about right." Jiggs sat down to eat. "Any time before that and he'll accuse drones of spying on his cattle."

26

"No need for spies in Two Pan. We've got our own. Roscoe Zalman told me Ox drove him off the road yesterday." Nap continued without noticing Jiggs shut his eyes and let out a long breath. "Gramps was puttering along their road, his head out the window, staring at the Zalman yearlings. He drove in the direction he was looking. Roscoe had to pull into the bar ditch and honk. Ox finally noticed and whipped around him. Miz Cleova says—"

"Hey!" Jiggs barked, like a tap on a horn to get someone's attention. "Just once, I'd like to start the morning without your grandfather ruining it."

The only noise that followed was the sound of forks clinking against plates. When Jiggs finished his eggs, he got up, squirted a dab of detergent onto his plate, and smeared it around with the sink brush. After a quick rinse, he laid it on a towel. "You do realize I hear those stories, too, don't you? There's a new dent in that old Chevy every other day." He also gave the skillet a bachelor wash and set it back on the stove. "Nobody will get his truck keys away from him until he's six feet under. He'll probably hide them before he goes."

Jiggs moved aside as Nap brought his plate to the sink. "When Roscoe's granddad started running over mailboxes, his family called the Oregon Highway Patrol. Officer Tripp came to their house and told the old man that destruction of mailboxes was a federal offense, and he owed some jail time. But Sheriff Meyer showed up and talked the sentence down. The old man had to turn over his keys and promise not to drive anymore. 'Course, it was all staged so his granddad wouldn't blame the family. Now every time the old codger sees Sheriff Meyer, he shoots him the finger. Right out in public. Shakes it at him."

Jiggs coughed a belly laugh. "I bet Sol's flipping the bird back, under the dashboard. That'll be me someday. That's what you've got to look forward to, Son."

"I'm putting you on Curly Dogs. Let your horse drive you."

"I haven't laughed in a long time. Thanks." Jiggs grinned. "So what're your plans today?"

Jiggs' smile faded. "I've gotta climb Starvation Ridge to look for Ox. He was pretty waspy last night—more than usual—when he heard the stream had dried up. He thinks someone's mining up there. We had supper together."

"I'm real sorry I missed that." A corner of Nap's mouth twitched up.

Jiggs studied his son. He had no idea why he was lucky enough to have a kid who'd turned out the way he had. He'd been a healing balm, doing little kindnesses for him after Katie had died. He'd bring a bug or flower or rock he'd found that he would've shown his mother if she'd been around. Together, they kept her memory alive.

"As usual," he slapped Nap's shoulder, "I said too much last night. I need to take a clue from my son's playbook and shut up, listen, then do what I want anyway."

Nap looked at him like he was crazy. "Good luck with that. You've got the same temper as Gramps."

"No, I don't. I used to, but that was before you were born. Now, I—"

Nap's head was bobbing as he pointed to his own face and his toothy, pasted-on smile. "This is what nodding, grunting, and not saying anything looks like." He turned and left.

Ox's pickup sat in the Starvation pasture to the west of the homestead. Jiggs parked next to it and followed the carved-out route of the streambed up the ridge. Rocks tipped beneath his feet as he hiked upward. He grabbed bushes to stay upright, climbing twenty yards. After a quick stop to catch his breath, he did it again, cursing himself for too many pies and donut holes.

He looked back over their property. His dad had bought other ranches when the owners had given up or died, but Starvation Creek was their biggest piece of land. Over a thousand acres. From this height, two dark gashes striping the pasture could be seen—ravines where the earth's crust had ripped as the ridge was being born.

A rock skittered past, bouncing downslope. He turned, searching for his father, but saw only big horn sheep watching from the boulders far above him. Jiggs scrambled upward, following a faint game trail zig-zagging through the sparse brush covering the hillside.

About a quarter mile up, next to the creek, he found an up-ended tree caving in the bank. The stream was now flowing into a strip of broken lava field. Most of the icy water trickled through the rocks and disappeared. Jiggs could hear it *gurgle* and *plink* as it rushed downhill—most likely in an ancient lava tube—underground. It was going to be a bear of a job to get water flowing back into the same creek. He looked around. There were no signs the big tree had been dynamited. No man was trying to "take their land" as Ox had insisted. It was only wind, time, and gravity—a rancher's old foes.

He took a different route back down the steep hillside. Each footstep made his knees ache with the impact. He scanned right and left, checking for snakes and half expecting to see Ox's body where he'd tuckered out, fallen, and hit his head. When he stopped to rest and wipe away sweat, he could smell the sage and bitterbush rising on the warm air from below. The Woolsey land rolled into the distance. Acres of grass struggled to grow in the latest drought. Cattle dotted the pasture between rocky outcroppings. A few bleached tumbleweeds nested against the stones. Above, there was more sky than a man knew what to do with. Below, a trail of dust rolled behind Ox's truck as it drove away.

"Hey!" Jiggs shouted, waving his arms, though he knew it would do no good. He quickly hurried down the hillside, grunting with each footfall. The dust trail had settled by the time he'd reached his truck. Jiggs whacked the fender with his hand, staring down the two-track path at the closed and locked gate. He turned and hurried to the old homestead spot.

The skull was gone. The flat stones had been stacked back into a row. A few new ones had been added. Footprints marked the sand. The sunlight made the same lacy patterns through the branches as it had the day before. A waxwing landed in the cottonwood and laughed a few notes. Time ticked by as usual. There was no evidence this place had ever been anything but a wide spot in a stream.

Jiggs puffed his cheeks and let loose a long breath. With an *ugggh*, he squatted in the dirt, his hands draped over his knees. Bound to happen. As usual, he'd been an idiot. He should've taken the skull last night and turned it in without saying a word. While he'd been up on the ridge, sweating and looking for Ox, the old fart had been down here, stealing the skull and tidying up.

Jiggs picked up a handful of pebbles, tossing the stones across missing water. They bounced and clattered downstream. Why would Ox do such a thing?

His fingers discovered the thin rock before his brain did. As he winged it away, his brain finally kicked him, asking what a jagged rock was doing among water-smoothed pebbles.

Clawing through the sand, he discovered a few more white fragments. He pushed aside a couple of flat stones. They hadn't been there yesterday. He was sure of it—and he'd had plenty of time to study all the rocks. Digging beneath them, he found a nest of bone fragments. Thin, curved pieces. Their broken edges unstained. Apparently, Ox hadn't stolen the skull after all. He'd stomped it to death.

Jiggs sat back in the sand. How did something so simple get so messed up? He should've been able to notify the authorities, get the skull off his land, and get on with life. But now...

He winged another pebble downstream. Either Ox was getting crazy in his old age, or the skull must carry more risk than he could imagine.

"Wealth is Like Dung, Useful Only When Spread"

—Chinese Proverb

JIGGS WENT HOME, but Ox wasn't there. Too many questions needed answers before telling the sheriff about the skull. They may have been childhood friends and rivals, but Sol took his sheriff duties seriously. Jiggs wanted to know what he was getting into before a truckload of museum curators or a van of forensic investigators pulled up at his house.

If his dad wouldn't talk, maybe Old Man Tower knew some history. As a boy, Jiggs had been told to stay clear of the crustiest, oldest geezer in the county. Near-blind and mostly nutty, the old galoot didn't know who he was talking to most of the time. He seemed to remember what happened years ago better than who he'd seen in the mirror that morning. He was long past the age of liking people, but tolerated them because they brought food or put plastic over his windows when the Boy Scouts needed a fall service project.

Located at the south end of Two Pan's Main Street, his shop was a museum of mechanics. Actually it was a junkyard, but he'd never turned in any scrap metal during either war. If a person was brave and brawny, he could hack through blackberry brambles and climb over mining jigs and timber cranes to find ore buckets filled with pickaxes—the handles rotted away. They were so rusty, like most things in the junkyard, they'd leave an orangey trail of metal flakes on any hand that touched them. The whole place was a lost tool shed, waiting for a distant generation to unearth the contents and wonder what they'd been used for.

Jiggs clanged the blackened brass bell, engraved *U.S.S. Cyclone,* hanging next to the entry. No one answered. He wrestled with the gate, which only opened a couple of feet before it stuck in the dirt. He shouldered past it and was circling a Tucker sedan when a voice rasped, "Get the hell out. I'm not open."

"Hey, Mr. Tower. It's Jiggs Woolsey. You remember me?"

"No!"

"How about my dad, Ox Woolsey?"

"Who wants to know?"

"I'm wondering if you have a bill hook for New Holland baler?" It was all Jiggs could come up with. He'd thought about stopping by before now and looking for one, but stories of a long afternoon with Old Man Tower had convinced him he had better things to do.

"Damn homesteaders," the codger mumbled and shuffled along a dirt path, squeezing through carts, horse-drawn wagons, and metal rip-rap. He kept up a steady hum of cursing, stopping suddenly next to a wooden box nailed to a tree. It used to house little brown forest bats, but now he pulled a machete out of it and jammed it into Jiggs hands. "Here. Make yerself useful. Don't make off with it. I know who you are."

"You do?" Jiggs followed him between stacks of car wheels.

"No, dammit." His voice soured. "Filled up on names. Don't give a damn. You're just another parts-pirate, wantin' somethin'. Here." He pointed to a mountain of blackberry vines. "Start hackin'."

"You're sure?" Jiggs wore a skeptical frown as he looked at the dense bramble.

The old man closed his eyes and waggled his head as he turned to shuffle away.

"All right. Hold on." Jiggs slashed and chopped, wishing he'd brought leather gloves. After fifteen minutes, the blade clanged against the faded-red metal of a New Holland baler. Jiggs stood back, wiping his arm across his forehead. "How did you remember where it was?"

"I live here. Where's yer tools? How you gonna get it out?"

Jiggs shook his head. "I wasn't expecting..." He raised his voice. "I'll be back. I'll borrow some tools from Bazz Hinton." The old man stared at him, his mouth slightly open. "The mayor?" Jiggs shouted. "Tools."

"That peckerhead." Old Man Tower shuffled off, mumbling, "I got spanners." Jiggs spent the wait-time cutting his way to the knotter box until he heard the mumble, "Nutcrackers and butt plugs," behind him. The old man shoved a wooden box of abused tools and a can of solvent at him, demanding, "Machete!"

Jiggs offered the handle. As soon as Old Man Tower grabbed it, he swung wildly at the vines. "Big dink of a stump," he rasped. " 'Round here somewhere."

"I'll do it. I'll do it!" When Jiggs had cleared vines from a stump, the old proprietor sat and rolled his hand, signaling *Get on with it*.

Jiggs sprayed nuts and bolts and banged on them, letting the oil get into threads. "Do you remember any of the Woolseys, sir?"

"You related to Ox Woolsey?"

"I am. He's my dad."

"He's a sonovabitch." With two fingers the old guy rubbed the white buildup from the corners of his mouth, and then pointed to a toilet leaning against a pile of dented fenders. "Check the tank."

Jiggs tilted the lid off the porcelain top and pulled out a bottle of clear liquid he was sure was moonshine. "This?"

The old man open and closed his fingers, signaling, *Gimme*. He took a drink then offered the bottle.

"No thanks. I gotta work." Jiggs looked upward, checking the sunlight filtering through the pines. He could tell this was going to be one of those *long* afternoons. Letting out a sigh, he took the bottle and slugged a drink. His throat turned to fire as "Oh...geez," croaked out.

The old man laughed, rocking back and forth. "You're not the lucky Woolsey. Bruno was." He took the bottle and tipped it to his lips again.

Jiggs' throat flamed once more from simply watching the man take a swig. He declined the bottle when offered this time. The alcohol loosened the old fossil's jaw muscles. His sentences became longer, his hand gestures livelier, and his cussing more colorful.

"Two things I heard 'bout your great-granddiddy."

Jiggs stopped trying to torque a bolt and looked at him.

"One...Bruno Woolsey was the luckiest bastard in the Oregon Territory."

"My great-grandad?" Jiggs' voice cracked as it limped its way out of his burning throat.

"Prussian army used to wear those damned hobnail boots. Big-ass, square-headed nails stickin' outta the soles. You seen 'em?"

Jiggs shook his head and went back to work. This is how it went with old nutcases. Their mouths worked while they wandered the lost rooms of their minds.

"I got a pair 'round here. Frightful bastards. You piss off one of them German officers, they'd scrape those boots down your shin. Peel off a quarter inch of hide. Sonsabitches. You could tell if a man was in the German army by his bloody legs."

He cursed several more times, finally noticing Jiggs working in the knotter box.

" 'Cept Bruno. Yer great-grandiddy hid on a ship. The nump sailed away."

Jiggs looked at him. "He was a stowaway?"

"The sailors went into the coal room and came out screaming. There was Bruno, head-to-toe, black with coal dust and only his eyes showin'. Most other ships woulda locked 'im in chains and sent his ass back, but that ship was bound for America. They patted him on the back, cleaned him up, and gave him small jobs to do. Lucky little shit."

Jiggs gave the old man a skeptical look and grabbed a mallet from the box.

"Hell, yes. That's the story he told my grandiddy." He nodded so hard, he clutched the stump to keep from falling off. " 'Course, when he got here, without papers and all, he found out he'd been pegged to join a New York Regiment to fight the Rebs."

"Must've been around 1860," Jiggs said.

" 'Spect so. He was just a pup. Fifteen or thereabouts. Cannon fodder. He didn't fight." The old man grinned. "Slipped off again, by damn. Joined a buncha pilgrims and drummers on the Oregon Trail. I guess he had quite a time of it. My great-granpap did too. It's prob'ly lies. Young men like to blow themselfs up big with tales. Never a problem for me. But it was true for Bruno. Seemed ever'thing he touched turned...well, it didn't turn to shit like it does for the rest of us." He took a drink and fell silent.

Jiggs let the quiet play out for a while. He'd gotten one nut loose and tapped on the other, trying to jar it without breaking it off. "So if Bruno told stories to your great-grandad, he must've made it to Oregon."

"What? Oh yuh. Fell in with some Irishman. You know what bogglers they are. I got some Irish blood. They can be

36

drinkers, but that never was a problem for me. 'Course, none of my kin seined more than a t'baccy sack of coarse gold outta the rivers. Bruno and his partner worked a placer claim over by Joseph. Produced a hunnerd ounces a day—so they said."

One of Jiggs' eyebrows rose. "I had a rich relative?" His voice was underlined with sarcasm.

Old Man Tower took another drink. "It was a wild place back then. Half-grown lad like that, pocketfuls of money. Luck riding his shoulders. He came to this side of the mountain and set several more claims. 'Course he was too rich to work. Hired Chinamen to tip the rockers while he pulled shenanigans and frequented Opal's Sporting Palace."

"His mines produced?" Jiggs said through clenched teeth, as he strained to pull the wrench handle.

The old man shrugged. "Never of heard any mine around here showing much color. Though there's folks still lookin'."

"I've never heard about any rich relations." Jiggs felt the nut give a little. He let go, whacked it three more times with a hammer, and grabbed the wrench again. "You said there were *two* things you knew about Bruno Woolsey. What's the other?"

"Yer granddiddy married the prettiest bedrocker in the whole damn whorehouse."

The wrench spun forward, smashing Jiggs' knuckles into the metal box before jerking loose and falling onto the tines below. He turned and looked at the shrunken old man sitting like a gnome on a stump. Tufts of yellowish-white hair circled his head. His thick glasses were so dirty, it was hard to see his bug eyes.

"Looks like ya got her loose." His grin showed only two front teeth.

"You're saying my great-grandmother was a whore?"

"I'm sayin' ever man in the territory considered Bruno the luckiest ball bag around. Money and opportunity kept chasin' after him. By then, the washouts from the Oregon Trail were leavin'. He snapped up land for cents on the dollar. 'Course, that was probably his hooker wife's doin's. She knew how to turn a buck. I don't think anybody called her a 'saloon gal' once they was married. She wore clothes fancier than the whores. She helped raise money for the Opera House and a few other hoity-toity places that don't exist anymore, thank the Lord. That's the damn way of women. My first wife, Adelia, used to spew and cuss like a split boiler if anyone said somethin' about her cooking. But if I misspoke a foul word now and then—"

"That was his first wife, right? He had others?" Jiggs interrupted.

"Oh hell, yes. I heard he was swingin' his wanker at every cat house and gentleman's club. He was a right pop'lar fella. A real storyteller."

"I mean..." Jiggs searched for words. "Did he have another wife who produced my grandfather...who I came from?"

"Nope." Old Man Tower shook his google-eyed head. "Ain't you heard family stories 'bout this?"

"None. Dad said he didn't know anything about the family. My granddad was too drunk to remember his own name, much less anybody else's. Nobody in town has ever mentioned it."

"Well, I can see why they'd leave out the part about her bein' a bride of the multitudes. Buncha bladdermouths. I can't even take a piss in front of my own shop without somebody givin' me hell. If I could get my stream goin' on command, I'd wet down their shoes while they're complainin'. Send 'em packin'."

Jiggs smiled to himself as he crawled under the baler to retrieve the wrench. The weaknesses of old age must be God's design to protect the rest of the populace from tired elderly cranks. He crawled out and mashed his bleeding knuckles into his jeans to stem the ooze. With his left hand, he finished taking off the nuts. "So how did I get here?"

"Helliky-damn, boy! If you don't know that, you're no kin to Bruno."

"I mean," Jiggs took a deep breath, "how do we get from Bruno to me? Who's in between?"

"Well, let's see..." He held the fifth up to the light and looked through the glass. Then he gave the liquid a hard shake. "Keeps the flavors stirred," he said when he saw Jiggs glance at him. He put a few drops of alcohol on his fingertip and rubbed it over his lips.

If the rot gut had any flavor, Jiggs couldn't tell. It had melted his taste buds. He willed himself not to ask why the old man was rubbing his lips with it. After years of listening to his dad, he'd learned that the best way to get out of the death grip of an old timer's story was not to ask any questions. Instead, he picked up a mallet and screwdriver and knocked the knotter prongs loose from the bolts.

"Bruno's wife gave him a son, Albrecht, your granddiddy. Only kid I know'd him to claim. Probably had a buncha bastards runnin' 'round, but none had his name or money."

"Crap!" Jiggs stared into the box. "Broke it."

"You ain't lucky like Bruno. I'm tellin' ya. He used it all up. When it was time for Albrecht to start school, his mama, being newly righteous with religion and social graces, took the kid and moved. St. Louie, I think. She never came back—what could be luckier for Bruno?"

Jiggs held up two pieces of the billhook.

"That's the crap for luck ya got now. You'll have to braze it." Old Man Tower stood up, waiting for a moment to see if he'd topple over. He shuffled to the toilet and put his bottle in the tank.

"What happened to Albrecht?" Jiggs picked up the tools and followed him.

"Shit. That poor kid didn't get a trace of good fortune or brains. Everbody called him 'Brick,' instead of Albrecht. He was that damn dumb. Didn't come back to Two Pan 'til he was growed. City life had ruined him by then. He mighta had a chance if Bruno was alive, but he'd passed on."

They reached the gate to the street. Jiggs had come for information, but it wasn't what he was looking for, and he was pretty sure the old fossil had twisted it up with his own family stories.

"I kid you not," the old man was yammering, but hanging back. "Brick was hard pressed to figure out which end of a horse grass went into."

"You know what?" Jiggs gave him the box of tools and pulled out his wallet. "I'm gonna call bull hockey on that one." He gave him a half grin. "What do I owe you?"

"Lemme tell ya..." The old man stepped forward and stood in the gateway, looking right then left before he spoke. "*Life* is bullshit." He waved at the junk behind him. "All of it turns back into dirt just like bull shit. And you don't owe me nuthin'. You got a broke billhook. What the hell would I do with it?"

Jiggs pulled a ten out of his wallet and stuffed it in the pocket of the old man's coveralls. He wouldn't dishonor the old buzzard by making him hold out his hand to take it.

He took a step toward his truck then hesitated. "Thanks for the stories about my great-granddad. You happen to know how Bruno died?"

"Prob'ly with a smile on his face."

"How about where he's buried?"

"Don't know. Nobody cares where you are after you're dead."

"Could be. I'm wondering...you've had this place a long time, haven't you?"

Old Man Tower stared at him and gave a single nod as though being this close to the street had dried up his speech.

"You ever find any bodies buried in there?"

"None of yer damn business." He slammed the gate with more force than Jiggs thought the old goat could've mustered.

"Promises and Pie Crusts Are Made To be Broken"

—Jonathan Swift

JIGGS GRUMBLED TO himself as he got into his truck. He needed to get home and fix leaky water pipes. Most of the day was gone, and he still didn't have an answer to the skull's identity or how it had gotten nested in his creek. The session with Old Man Tower had barely been profitable. He'd gleaned a broken baler part and the name of a relative. Too bad he'd probably never be able to taste anything again. Remembering the morning's climb, his stomach told him he'd skipped lunch—not that he couldn't stand to miss a few meals.

Driving down Two Pan's Main Street, he passed Hermes, the town donkey, ambling along the roadway and surrounded by five kids wearing backpacks. Morning and afternoons the neddy could be seen escorting children to school.

He pulled to a hard stop in front of the Two Pan Bar and Grill. As he got out of his truck, a pigtailed girl about four feet tall called, "Mr. Woolsey. Wait!" A round-cheeked boy in the pack, yanked on the donkey's harness, with a *Whoa!*

The donkey ignored him, making the kid dance alongside until the animal clopped to a stop in front of Jiggs.

"Is this what you kids want?" Jiggs rattled the coffee can hanging from the rafters of the Bar and Grill's overhang.

"Yes, sir. Thank you." She looked at him with the confidence that comes from everyone knowing where she lived, who her parents were, and all three of her given names. And if disaster did strike, like falling out of a tree or getting fingers pinched in a door, someone would come to her rescue.

Hermes had no patience for politeness. He U-shaped his neck to stick it in the can.

"Hyaa!" Jiggs pulled it away, disapproval in his voice. The kids laughed. He held the can toward them. Several hands dove in, pulling out broken chunks of donkey cubes. "Just one, everybody. He's getting fat."

He scratched the neddy's head while the kids flat-palmed the treats in front of donkey teeth. He stuck the can back under the eaves and went inside to a chorus of *Thank you, Mr. Woolsey* and *Bye, Mr. Woolsey*. It felt good, though he couldn't say quite why. He wondered if Old Man Tower had ever heard his name called with such enthusiasm, or did he only hear people yell at him?

Sliding onto a seat at Table 2, he studied the walls to see if any new "history" had been added to the ragtag display of boots, lariats, axes, and miners' headlamps. Like the junkyard, the walls showed the rise and fizzle of the town and its residents.

"Hey." A twenty-two-year-old blonde rapped the table. It wasn't so much of a greeting as Misty's method to keep from repeating herself. She made sure you were tuned in when she spoke, because she wasn't going to say it twice. "You're late for lunch. Early for dinner. So...are you here for beer?"

"I think I just drank kerosene. What do you have that'll take the taste out of my mouth?"

"Light a match and swallow it," Basil Hinton said as he sat down at the "news" table, cleverly marked Table 2 by a tiny plastic sign. He'd only lived in Two Pan ten years, but enjoyed resident privileges such as folks shortening his name to Bazz, being elected mayor because no one else wanted the job, and being on the receiving end of pranks.

"I had a drink with Old Man Tower. Do I still have lips, or have they melted, too?"

"How about a chocolate milkshake?" Misty asked.

"You'd do better with Junior's new dinner special," Bazz said. "It'll cure your ills. It's a soothing fruit mousse—"

"Stop it, Dad," Junior growled as he walked by in his long black apron. "I've told you before. I don't start dinner until five." He moved his accusing stare from his father to Jiggs. "Don't feed the donkey in front of my door. He drops a load every time. I keep moving that damn treat can. Somebody keeps putting it back."

"Guess it'll only be the milkshake." Jiggs glanced at Misty and returned the plastic menu to its spot between the salt and pepper shakers.

"And that's how you lose sales," Bazz said to his son. "But what do I know? I only bought this falling down saloon and built it into—"

"A burger shack. That's all it was. And a stockpile of redneck knickknacks." Junior slung gestures toward the artifacts that the residents had brought in. "I'm surprised you don't have the two mining pans this burg was named after, but I'm sure somebody will drag them in."

Jiggs leaned back and studied Junior. "You haven't quite got over leaving Los Angeles, have you? What's it been? A month?"

"Seems like twenty years."

"Misty," Jiggs called when he saw the waitress walking toward them. "Tell our newest resident how the town got its name."

44

She slid the funnel-shaped glass and frosty metal cup with the extra milkshake across the table. "I don't give tourist talks. Either order something else or clam up. I've got a job to do." She walked to the long walnut bar and began quartering limes.

"There." Junior pointed at the waitress. "There's the reason sales are down."

"She was here before you, and sales were fine," Bazz said. "You'll go before she does."

Junior threw up his hands. "But I own the place now."

"Then you should know…" Jiggs said, "miners couldn't find two pans worth of gold here. That's how this wide spot got its name."

"Oh." Junior turned his attention to the customer coming through the door. His body stiffened, and then he barreled across the room calling, "No you won't." Millie cringed as he came at her, but he squeezed past and kept going.

The sound of his shouting drifted into the bar as she held the door open, looking outside. Jiggs sat back, spooning milkshake into his mouth. "Who's he hollering at?"

The frizzy-haired woman gave the group a sad frown. "Potty. You know, I feel sorry for that ol' dog. It's rangy and stinks, but it keeps turning circles, looking for a place to lie down."

Bazz propped both elbows on the table, rubbing his hands over his face as he let out a long sigh.

Millie hurried from the door to take a seat. A moment later Junior walked in, striding with purpose toward the telephone behind the bar.

"Feel better now?" Jiggs asked.

"I'm calling Animal Control. I've got a crapping donkey and a flea-bitten mutt infesting the front of my restaurant."

Misty snorted a laugh. Jiggs grinned.

"What?" Junior looked at one then the other. "I suppose this broke-back town doesn't have anyone."

"It's me," Bazz said, staring at the ceiling, consciously avoiding his son's gaze. "Mayor, dog catcher, traffic control. I do it all. Fix a hot dog for the mutt. That's an official order."

Junior's eyes shot daggers at him before he stormed toward the kitchen. "I'm *not* feeding that dog."

"Hey, that sounds good. I'll take two," Jiggs called after him.

"Of course you would. Damn carnie-food..." The rest of Junior's grumble was lost as he disappeared into the kitchen.

"I'd say he's got a ways to go before he falls in love with this place." Jiggs used his spoon to help the milkshake slide from the metal cup into his glass.

Bazz stared at the kitchen door. "I think it's more of a father-son thing. We get in each other's way a lot."

"Boy howdy. I know that story." They were silent a minute, each man mulling through his thoughts. Jiggs finally said, "Get a load of this. According to Old Man Tower, I come from big money."

"That nutbag?" Bazz shook his head. "I barred him from this place. Used to cuss and insult the customers." Bazz glanced at the kitchen. "That's Junior's job now. He's good at it. So where'd all your money go, Daddy Warbucks?"

"Don't know. Petered away on fine living by one of my forbears, I think. Dad doesn't talk about family. The only thing he's ever said was that his father was a weak-willed drunk who died on the day I was born. Mom said he was simply a sick, tired old man. She liked to tell me Granddad handed me the baton of life as we passed each other coming through the celestial portals. Dad said he handed me a shitstick."

Bazz nodded. "That'd be your dad."

"Say," Jiggs looked up, "are there still death records at the Opera House?"

Bazz gazed at him a moment. "Sure." He smiled. "Go over there and have a look. You don't need a key. It's open right now."

"Isn't Tracy..." Misty began, but Bazz nailed her with a quick stare. Jiggs glanced back and forth between the two.

Bazz slapped the table with a *bang*, shaking his head. "Believe it or not, Old Man Tower once brought me a piece of Two Pan memorabilia. It was too repugnant, even for me."

"You're right. That's hard to believe." Junior frowned as he delivered two hotdogs in paper trays.

Bazz ignored his son. "It was a doorbell for the bar. A taxidermist had stuffed the back half of an antelope. That's all there was, hind feet and a tail that stuck straight up. Someone had wired it so the doorbell's push button was in the butt."

Misty rolled her eyes. "And people wonder why I don't like to talk at work."

"On that thought...I think I'll go." Jiggs picked up his hotdogs as he stood. "Tower probably wanted you to have it because he doesn't like you. Calls you a peckerhead."

"I'd agree with that," Junior said and turned to Jiggs. "You want any relish or mustard for your kid's meal?"

"If you'd encourage customers to stay, they'd order more," Bazz said.

"More junk. With wads of fake cheese," Junior sneered. Jiggs went out the door, leaving father and son in a heated discussion over cholesterol.

He ate as he strolled along the boardwalk. At the end of the walkway, he thudded down the steps, stopping by the dog lying in the weeds at the side of the building. The mutt lifted its snout, catching the scent of food. Through rheumy eyes, it watched him cross the street and throw trash in a can. When he'd disappeared into a building, the old hound tentatively licked the hotdog he'd put between its paws.

*

47

In its day, the Two Pan Opera House had been a gem of the West. The thick granite walls were quarried from the flanks of the Eagle Caps. Teams of freight wagons had hauled the ornate stage and padded velvet seats over the mountains.

Seeing no cars around, Jiggs climbed freshly-cured concrete steps. The Daughters of Two Pan had been at it again, keeping the old place alive. He tried to avoid both the building and the Daughters. A pleasant conversation could become a hitch, roping a man into more work than he'd ever imagined.

Inside, his footsteps echoed as he crossed the stone floor. The auditorium, no longer filled with stage, stairs, or seats, sent sound bouncing from wall to wall.

He stepped into the cozy backstage space. It had been made into a conference room by placing the original twelve-foot oak doors on sawhorses, providing a table during city council meetings. Wooden file cabinets leaned against the walls. He wasn't quite sure what he was looking for. He'd take a quick tour of the 1860s to see if he could find any Woolseys, how they died, and where they were buried. He checked his watch.

Some of the files didn't have dates, but he could suss out the timeline. Unfortunately, no amount of heaving or yanking would open a drawer. None of them. Seated on the floor, his feet braced against other cabinets, he pulled and threatened to "use a blow torch on all of you." His grunting complaints obscured the footsteps of Tracy, the feed store lady. She watched from the doorway a moment before asking, "Good heavens. What're you doing?"

Jiggs thought it was obvious, but after climbing a mountain, digging for crushed skull, peeling his knuckles off, and poisoning himself with hooch, he was pretty sure he wasn't in the best of moods. He let out a long breath, discarding his first response. Instead, he opened and closed his fist a few times to get blood pumping back into his fingers after gripping drawer handles.

Tracy watched him without saying a word or moving.

Finally Jiggs looked up, a flatline smile on his face that expressed no joy. "Can I help you?"

"Is your dad all right?"

Jiggs groaned slightly as he pushed off the floor and stood. "Why? What's he done now?"

"Your feed bill is overdue."

"That can't be right." He frowned.

"Well, you know how Ox usually comes in and pays it on the last Tuesday of every month? I haven't seen him. It's six weeks past. Is he okay?"

"Cranky as usual. I'm sorry, Tracy. I'll write you a check. We keep different accounts, but he insists on paying the bills. I don't know if I'll ever get the ranch checkbook away from him."

"No, don't pay me. He'll be upset. He likes to pay face to face, pinching the feed sacks and cussing about the world for a half hour. I think he saves up topics. It's his entertainment. I said something so you'd mention it to him. Would you?"

"I'd rather pay you myself than have that conversation. Have you called him?"

"He can't hear a thing on the phone. Keeps yelling, 'Who?'"

"Have you sent out a bill?" She nodded, staring at him. "Okaaaaaay," Jiggs said slowly. "I'll talk to him. But I've got several hot topics that come before yours. He may have stormed out of the room by the time I get to your bill, and I'll be sitting there, talking to myself."

"Like you were just now?"

"That's different. These are supposed to be accessible."

"Those haven't been opened since Lillie Langtry was here. They warped so badly the files were moved to the county courthouse."

Jiggs glanced at his watch. "Well, I'm not sure why Bazz sent me over here, but thanks. If you'll excuse me, I've got to make a run to Enterprise." He squeezed past her.

"You don't want to go out that way," she said.

"There you are!" Tricia Kruger called across the hall. "We were looking for you."

"I tried to warn you," Tracy said quietly.

"Come out here, Jiggs, and look at the new steps," Tricia called. "We need your opinion on the handrail."

He knew what that meant. Every man in Two Pan had been snookered by that phrase. Katie had been a member of the Daughters of Two Pan. He dearly missed his wife, but he didn't regret losing the weekly nagging about the unending list of chores the Daughters had for every husband.

"I'm in a hurry right now, Tricia. I need to get over to Enterprise." He looked at the sky as they walked outside. The daylight seemed to be marching forward without any promise of slowing down.

She ignored him, fanning her hand toward the brackets and pile of lumber. "We don't know where to begin."

"I liked the old steps. Blocks of quarried granite. Matched the building. Had character."

"They did. You're right." She leaned down and rubbed a copper penny—date side up—that someone had pressed into the concrete as it had cured. "But they were so old and used that a dip had worn in the middle of each tread. Can you imagine how many people passed through to wear them down like that?"

She left no room for an answer, continuing on, "Water collected and froze in the tops. It was a lawsuit looking for a home. Now we have a safe, new entrance that needs a handrail. Please? We've got a whole peach pie we could pay you with. We were over at Tracy's taking a break. We've been working all afternoon. We plan to put up pictures..."

Jiggs held up his hand, looking at his watch. "I'll look at it on one condition. Nobody talks to me. It's been that kind of day. I want peace and quiet. Pound the heck out of something and get going."

"Oh!" Tricia blinked. She held up her hand and backed off. "I understand completely. I'm going to run over to Grubbs and get you some ice cream to go with that pie."

"No, thanks. I appreciate it, but I don't need it. I do need to get some tools though. If you're not here when I get back, I'll work on it tomorrow."

"No problem. The mayor dropped off what you'll need." Tricia grinned at him.

Jiggs glanced at the house next to the Two Pan Bar and Grill. Bazz waved from the front porch.

"He came by Tracy's about five minutes ago. Told us you were here and left these tools."

Jiggs looked at the sky again. What he needed was to get to the records at Enterprise before he confronted his dad tonight. And he needed better friends. "Excuse me a minute," he said, walking with purpose toward the mayor's house.

Logic Has Left The Barn

"THAT WAS A skunkdog trick." Jiggs threatened to bend, scar, and soak Bazz's tools in water. He stood on the sidewalk, trying to think of more tool abuse; then it dawned on him that spouting threats from ground level was like a slave cussing Caesar in the coliseum; so he climbed the eight steps of the former cat house to bully the man eye to eye.

By the time Tricia Kruger got there, the men were drinking beer, rocking in the porch swing, and complaining about something else. "Mr. Woolsey?" She cocked her head slightly to the side like she was looking around a corner as she walked toward them.

Jiggs recognized this classic gesture: she was going to ask questions, and she already knew the answers to each one. He wondered why women did it. Probably they thought it produced shame. She spoke with a smile. "When you didn't come back, we assumed you'd left for Enterprise. You said you were in quite a hurry."

Jiggs hesitated. There wasn't a question in there. Usually, the "scolding quiz" was easy. A woman asked a question. He figured out the correct answer. Then he compared it with what he'd actually done, which was usually the opposite—thus, the shame. But she hadn't asked a question. However, her tone was undeniably, *What the hell are you doing*? He cleared his throat. "Uh, yeah. I needed to make a call. I don't carry a cell phone."

"That's amazing in this day." She crossed her arms.

Bazz shook his head. "You're a really bad liar. I *know* you don't have a phone, and that didn't even convince me. How about saying, 'Jugenmeir is changing pastures. About seventy-five cows are blocking the road to Enterprise,' or 'Everything would've been closed by the time I got there'?"

Jiggs squinted at him. "I don't need your assist with excuses. And I don't think that's what she's saying. Did George really move cows today? Without help?"

Tricia Kruger watched the men wander the conversation in a different direction. She was amazed how dense guys could be. Or maybe that was their master tactic. By "not getting it," they got out of a lot of work. She thought about going up the steps to continue her request, but decided her strategy would be more effective from the "disadvantaged" lower position. Her eyes scanned the two Hefeweizen bottles under the swing and the two in their hands. She focused on Jiggs and began, "Were you going to finish the job today?"

He smiled. Finally a question! He knew the correct answer, but replied, "No," anyway. He figured he might as well skip the dancing and go right to God's honest truth.

"Oh!" Her expression flattened.

"It's really a two-man job." Jiggs nodded, confirming his own opinion, and then hooked a thumb toward the mayor, who was taking a long pull on his bottle. "And Bazz doesn't want to start on it—obviously." Tricia Kruger's eyebrows rose. "What's your husband doing right now?" Jiggs asked.

"Kent had to take some calves over to Colfax." Her voice had pushback. "Then he—"

"He doesn't want to do it either." Jiggs held eye contact with her. "You get that. Right?"

"None of us *want* to be spending all day arguing about what pictures go where or patching an old building, only to have a different part fall off." She stared at Jiggs, centering him in her sights as though she were looking down a shotgun barrel.

He knew that look. His mother used to whip Ox with it. Words would gallop out fast, stepping on the one before. It didn't really matter what was being said. It was the tone. Sharp and accusing. His mother had never cussed. She hadn't needed to. She'd smack Jiggs and Pax for every foul word she'd heard them utter right up into their teens—then she had died. And everything went to hell.

He watched Tricia Kruger wave her hands, palms up like she was lifting heavy objects. She kept up a steady flow of "what-ifs." She'd have a heck of a time settling down tonight. As Ox used to say, "Logic has left the barn."

Tricia was pointing now. "It needs to be done. And what if we all felt that way? What would happen to this town then?"

Jiggs stood while she was still talking. He drained his beer then interrupted because he sensed no gap in her word traffic. "Yes it does."

"What? What did you say?"

He shrugged. "You're right. It needs to be done." He nodded toward Bazz. "You got me into this. Let's go finish it."

She turned and tromped toward the Opera House. Her steps quickened upon seeing the other women get in cars and trucks and pull away. "Oh great, everyone's leaving now."

"Even better," Jiggs mumbled as he and Bazz followed.

Tricia flagged down ladies and handed out additional duties. Bazz picked up his hammer, testing the weight of it in his hand. "You know, there's a reason women aren't beating down your door, and you're not married again. When Tricia tells the other ladies about this, she'll be referring to you as 'jackass.'"

"That's not the reason, I haven't remarried." Jiggs examined a cedar 2X2. "But being a jackass is better than being a peckerhead."

The men measured, cut, and hammered. Thanks to Tricia driving away, they worked without interruption. Thanks to the world tilting toward the sun, the daylight decided not to shut down until half past eight. When they finished at 10 p.m., they headed to the Bar and Grill for supper and shared the pie. Jiggs saved two slices for Nap and Ox.

When he got home that night, the lights were off in Ox's house. He beat on the door anyway. "We've got to talk about what you did this morning. And I know why the creek dried up." Ox didn't answer.

"I'm not going to stand on the stoop and talk through the door."

But he was.

"I've got peach pie." It was unfair to bait the old guy like that. It was like putting peanut butter on a squirrel trap. "It's homemade."

And yet...there was still no answer.

Jiggs was up early the next morning, pounding on Ox's door again. "If you don't show yourself, I'll have to break in to see if you're dead."

After a minute the curtain moved aside. The old man scowled through the glass. Jiggs stood on the porch, hands on his hips, waiting in the gray-pink dawn. Ox turned away and left him standing there. "We need to talk. I'm staying 'til you come out." He parked himself on the low stoop, stretching his legs into the gravel drive in front of him and organizing his day. He'd spent twenty-four hours and was no closer to finding out who'd once worn the skull or why they'd left it on Starvation Ridge. And why did it matter? He should tell Sol about it and let him "sheriff" it out. That's what he was paid for.

Jiggs thoughts were stuck. There was a deeper secret inside that cranium. One that hinted its existence shouldn't be trumpeted into the light of day. He glanced over his shoulder to see if his dad was watching through the window. He wasn't. But clearly, there was something about the skull that Ox hated. Maybe it was the reason Ox rarely mentioned family. "Hey!" Jiggs called out. "You know anything about Bruno Woolsey?" There was no noise from the house.

"Then I'm going over to the courthouse," he yelled. "Look him up and nose around in the records." Involving the government should've brought Ox storming outside, but there was still no sound.

It didn't take long for Jiggs' mind to wander to leaky faucets, broken gates, getting water back in a stream, and the hundred things he had to do today. He stood up and dusted off his jeans. He was a fool. He never could wait long, and his father knew it. "We'll talk tonight. That's for certain," he yelled.

Nap leaned out the door of the big house, a slice of pie in his hand. "Who're you talking to?"

"Who do you think lives here?" Jiggs' voice was thorny.

"Well, Gramps just rode out the back of the barn."

"Craphouse crickets!" Jiggs jumped off the porch and rounded the house. A big blue roan trotted toward the back pasture. Ox sat atop like he was part of the horse.

"What are you two fighting about now?"

"Nothing." Jiggs followed his son into the house. "You can have your granddad's piece of pie."

"Thanks." He held up the empty pan. "Are we working on the water tank and lines at Blank Map this morning?"

"I need to make a quick dash to Enterprise first."

"For?"

Jiggs stared at him. If there was something criminal about the skull, it would be better for Nap not to be involved. Besides, the more people who knew of it, the harder it was to control the ballyhoo. "Creech Walters. I'm meeting him for breakfast."

"You hang out with too many windbags."

Jiggs hadn't really intended to stop at Walters' Sporting Goods, but after leaving the courthouse at Enterprise, he was spitting mad. He needed to talk to a sane person. The small wood-shingled shop was outfitted with walls of fishing rods, bins of arrows, and shelves of camouflage hunting accessories. A sign hung over the hand-tied flies "Guaranteed NOT to catch fish. But will look GREAT in your tackle box."

In the back room, a padded work table sat beneath spotlights as though it were an operating arena. Jiggs drew a deep breath as he walked through the door. The place always carried the musk of deer lure, gun oil, beef jerky and dust.

"Woolsey!" The thick-bodied owner called. "What brings you 'round? I'm all out of money, so you can't rob me today."

"Guess I'll have to wait 'til you get a high roller to guide into the wilderness. How about we go to the Minam Cafe for a cup? I need to pick your brain about a problem."

"Got coffee here. Don't have too much brain."

Jiggs poured himself a mugful and settled in a fat armchair covered with ranch brands. "It starts with Old Man Tower telling me that my great-granddaddy struck it rich."

"He once told me Kaiser Bill was his relative."

"In either case, the money is long gone for both of us, so don't ask him or me for a loan. But it got me wondering where my great granddad ended up. So I went to the courthouse, looking for death records. The gal working the counter said Oregon didn't hand out certificates for the accomplishment of dying in those days. She found his name listed in the town registry, but that was all. It doesn't say where he was buried or how he went. So I'm back to the start-end of the rope, trying to figure out where to look."

Creech had stirred his coffee as he listened. He took a sip then raised his eyebrows as though sharing a secret. "You want help with places to look, huh, Woolsey? You think his gold is buried with him?"

"No. No. I doubt if there's any money. I'd simply like to know my great-granddad's final resting place."

"I'd say there're plenty of pioneer cemeteries around here. Some of them haven't even been discovered yet."

"You're almost as helpful as the clerk. We'd been looking through old registries for fifteen minutes when she said, 'What was your name again?' I wondered what name she'd been looking for. She could've overlooked Bruno, but when I told her 'Woolsey,' then she dropped the bombshell." Jiggs paused to let his words gain a little weight.

"She looked up, tapping her temple with a pencil and said, 'That's really interesting. There was a man in here last week, looking up property records on an O-A-C-H-S Woolsey.' She spelled it out."

"I told her. 'That's my dad. 'Course, everybody calls him Ox.' "

"Why're they looking up your property?" Walters asked.

"That's what I wanted to know. When I posed the question, she told me, 'They don't have to give a reason to check documents.' She was real snippy and not particularly helpful when I asked more questions. Wouldn't even say what the fella looked like."

"So how do you need my help? Are you looking for your dead granddad or figuring out who's checking up on your property?"

"I'm pretty steamed someone's digging through my records. You're a successful business man. I thought you'd see things clearer than me right now. There're too many weird events falling on top of each other. The stream dried up on Starvation Creek. Then I find out I had rich ancestors. Someone is snooping through my land files. And Ox thinks we might have a poaching prospector around our place, but we don't."

"Look Woolsey, we may have to call in a few consultants, attorneys, and an expert on whale mating. Can you afford all that, or are you willing to accept my experienced opinion?"

"I can always ignore anything you say, and your coffee's free, so go ahead."

"Give up the search for Grandpa, unless you want to drive to every graveyard in the U.S. He may not even be buried with a headstone. Maybe his spot is marked with an old plank cross, and it's already rotted away. Are you sure he's not relaxing at God's Hollow?"

"No." Jiggs stared into his cup. "I go out there every other month. I know all the Woolsey headstones."

"Sorry, Jiggs, I didn't mean to bring up old wounds. I'm afraid you've hit a dead end with great-granddad. The prospector, on the other hand is easier. I've got deer cameras you could rig up to prove to Ox there's no claim jumper. Even if you had one, he's not getting much. The only people who're getting gold are using big dredges over by Joseph. And I think I can shed a little light on the land records." Walters pushed out of his chair, got the coffee pot, and warmed up their drinks.

"Last fall, I guided a group of doctors on an elk-hunting trip. Big spenders. They'd been to eastern Oregon before. Loved the high desert, the remoteness, and the pace. One of them was champing at the bit to buy a ranch."

"Tell them nothing's for sale. We've got enough valley people here."

"One fella told a story about hunting here two years ago before they started hiring me. He didn't bother to get an elk tag. So when a guy in his group yelled, 'Game ranger coming,' this numb-nut threw a two thousand dollar rifle over the cliff at Creek View so he wouldn't get fined or barred from hunting. Bragged about it to the whole group."

"Maybe I should have a look around the base of Creek View."

"Don't bother." Walters nodded toward his workroom. "It was rusty, but cleaned up fine. I think your courthouse snoop was a realtor scrabbling to put together a real estate deal. Did they look at other properties?"

"The clerk was sparse with information."

"Well, there you go. You're not rich. Nobody's gonna get rich mining your land. If your forefathers did strike it rich—they and the money are both long gone. And if someone wants to buy those acres your daddy's collected, then maybe you'd be rich again. That's it. Glad to be of service. I'll send you my bill." Walters sat back and took a drink of coffee.

"That only leaves one more problem." He set his cup on a barrel, buying time to frame his words. "You ever find anything...out of place...in the woods? Something that shouldn't have been there?"

"Hah! Ran across a marijuana patch once. Hightailed it right back out. Why? What did you find?"

Jiggs looked at him, weighing his words. It seemed wrong to ask a guy for advice and not tell him what it was actually about. But what if the skull was something that should've never surfaced? A family secret. Or what if he was making a big fuss and winding up the rumor mill over dead family? "I found an...old timepiece. Gold. No initials or identifying marks," he said. "It doesn't work."

Walters gave Jiggs knowing look. "Sure. You looking to sell it?" When Jiggs shook his head, he continued, "I've got a jeweler here in Minam. He might be able to get it cleaned up. Tell you more about it."

"That's good to know. I doubt if I'll ever find the owner, but it makes me want to know its story." Jiggs looked at his watch. He'd learned possible information about who was snooping into his land records, but he was still where he started with the skull.

"Now, Woolsey, tell me more about your family striking it rich."

"Tower said my great-grandmother was a hooker."

Walters put his feet on an ottoman and settled deeper into his chair. "He's crazier than a run-over dog. You can't believe a word he says."

Jiggs agreed and drained his coffee, but in the back of his mind he was sure there was a thread of truth haunting the story. Why else would Ox do a stomp dance on the skull?

"Nobody Ever Drowned in His Own Sweat"

—Ann Landers

JIGGS DROVE SLOWLY to avoid the dust Nap's Dodge kicked up as they traveled down the driveway. They'd spent the afternoon working on pipes and the water tank. Jiggs had carefully avoided the subject of family. Ox was the only one who could give him the explanation he wanted.

Because the old man was avoiding him, Jiggs had come up with a new plan. Unfortunately, it required more time and patience. It was like approaching a wild horse, he'd have to keep the old guy calm but distracted before he could catch some answers.

From half-way down the drive, he could see sawhorses and lumber in front of the small house. Ox's tall, stoop-shouldered frame was bent over a project, his hand pumping a hammer. As they parked, the old man looked at Jiggs with a warning scowl then went back to work.

"What'cha doin?" Nap asked as he slammed his truck door.

"Makin' something to sit on, so's I can watch for coyotes."

"Why don't you use a patio chair?"

Ox straightened, looked at his grandson, and waited for him to figure out the answer. When the young man didn't say anything, Ox picked up an electric saw. "Maybe those fat-cushioned chairs are bothersome to lift out of. Maybe I don't wanna drag a hard chair from the kitchen every time I wanna sit. Or maybe I feel like making something with my hands. Pick any one you want."

Nap's eyebrows arched as he said, "Okaaay."

"You want some cheap help?" Jiggs asked.

"I know how to make a damn bench." He revved the saw, its pitch singing higher as he pushed it through a pencil line on a treated 2x4.

Jiggs and Nap exchanged glances. When the whirring squeal of the saw died down, Jiggs said, "You taught me about woodwork. I thought you could teach Nap a thing or two." Ox grunted. Jiggs took that as a good sign. He hadn't commented how Jiggs couldn't cut a straight corner with a handsaw.

"That's okay, Gramps. I took shop in school."

"Whad'ya make?" Ox looked up.

"A storage case for DVDs."

"I don't know what that is, but it sounds like a foot-long project. Pick up a hammer. I'll show you how to make something man size that requires more than two tools."

Jiggs held up a white paper sack. "I picked up fried chicken at Slat's GasNGo. You want some?"

"Yeah," Ox mumbled.

In a half hour, the men were sitting on the patio behind the big house, raking potato salad out of containers. For Jiggs, the meal had the same tense feeling as sitting at school, waiting for the bell to ring. He picked his topics carefully. He and Nap discussed working on the waterlines at Blank Map. Ox ate and listened, giving one word comments, when he spoke at all.

"Hey, I never told you why the water dried up at Starvation Creek." Out of the corner of his eye he saw Ox stiffen with a drumstick paused half-way to his mouth. "It was an uprooted tree." Jiggs went on to tell what he'd discovered, never mentioning the skull or that Ox had been nearby.

It was a technique he'd learned from his mom. She was a tall woman, but Ox was taller. Yet at times, she seemed towering and more powerful. She wouldn't out-cuss Ox, but she could out talk him. There was no way she could push him over, so she had the cleverest ways of mining the argument around him, and he'd cave in. If they were arguing, she'd circle the topic like a wolf, coming near it, but not quite touching upon it. It wore Ox down. He'd become as wary as a rabbit, never knowing if she was going to leap into the quarrel or let it slide until another day.

Jiggs ignored his father's guarded looks. By the time the Woolsey men were discussing how to fix the dried up stream, Ox had become talkative. He and Nap had teamed up behind the idea of dynamiting the channel back into place.

"Who knows what problems that'll cause? The whole ridge might come sliding down. You just want to see something blow up." Jiggs was surprised to find himself on the side of reason, arguing with two people who were grinning like kids waiting for a fireworks show.

"If we're not demolishing the hillside, then I've got other plans." Nap stood and picked up his plate. "It was a *good* dinner." The tone of his words made it an evaluation of their time together rather than about the food.

"It was," Jiggs agreed. Ox nodded.

The sun had dipped below the horizon. Darkness collected in the corners around the ranch. The breeze had quieted. Not a leaf stirred. A few birds called from the roost they'd found for the night. Black silhouettes of trees stood against a bruised sky. No one spoke through the "still moment" as light and time seemed to slow to a near stop. Then Venus glowed, nudging the world to roll on, pick up speed as more heavenly bodies made their appearance.

The aroma of lilacs floated in the air. Ox closed his eyes. The floral scent reminded him of other years when the boys were little and they worked late and ate on the patio, watching the stars. It was easier to tell them things back then. They listened.

"Well..." he sighed, opening his eyes, He hadn't had such a pleasant evening in a long time. Usually, he ate alone or arguing with Jiggs. It wasn't clear why that happened, besides the fact that Jiggs had always been a hard-headed kid. Ox pushed leg bones to the center of his plate and wadded his napkin into a ball. Time to leave before the conversation turned sour.

"Hey, I learned something yesterday," Jiggs said, patting his belly and leaning back as though he were settling in.

Ox froze. Warning bells went off in his head. He either needed to duck incoming bricks or start hurling his own stony accusations. "What's that?" he mumbled.

"I stopped by Old Man Tower's. Picked up a part for the baler."

"Yeah?" He turned and stared into the sunset that had disappeared. Something else was coming.

"He told me Bruno Woolsey struck gold in these parts."

Ox closed his eyes, pushing Jiggs' voice away. He remembered when Tower had dark hair, a pencil neck, and big ears sticking off the sides of his head. Unconsciously, he reached up and pulled at what was left of his own ear. Tower was older than him by ten years and still trying to rub spit in his hair after all this time.

"You know any stories about him?" Jiggs interrupted his thoughts. It must've been the second time he'd said it, because he'd clicked up his voice a notch.

"I remember one occasion," Ox said, "when I was driving a team and wagon down Main Street. We'd—"

"Here in town?"

"Hell, yes, here in town. Where else do you think I'd be? New York City?" He stared Jiggs into silence. "We'd used horses to pull a danky stump from in front of the Lutheran church. I was hauling it off in the wagon. Tower was sitting in front of their establishment. Back then it was an automotive-mechanic shop. Now it's a dump. Anyway, he was propped on the back legs of his chair, gawkin' and doing nothing, as usual. Big McGinty drove by in his new Hudson Commodore and honked. My horses startled, jerking one way then the other. I fell off the wagon still hangin' onto the reins. It was a tangled mess, but I didn't let 'em run.

"Tower thought it was the funniest thing he'd ever seen. The lazy cuss was still laughing when I picked him up by the collar and told him, 'A man who's workin' can expect to get scrapes and scars. If you sit on your butt all the time, you'll never get hurt.'"

Jiggs nodded. "That's what you said whenever we got maimed. Even when the tractor rolled over my foot. So, what did Tower do?"

"Bled. I punched him in the face."

"That explains a lot. I guess you didn't hear me, but what I actually asked for was stories about Bruno Woolsey, who, according to Old Man Tower, was my rich great granddaddy."

"I can't believe the bastard is still trying to goad a Woolsey about that." Ox's stare hardened. "Tower tried to taunt me with the same thing a couple of times. He liked to sneer about losing all that money, as though it made him better. I've had to sock him more than once over the years."

"Is the gold story true?"

"Does it matter? Are you any better off today because some relative had money? I didn't see any of it. There was land. That's a fact. It's also true that everything my dad touched turned to shit. He never talked about family when he was sober. I didn't believe anything he said when he was drunk."

"So you don't know if Bruno Woolsey was your grandfather or where he's buried?"

"Oh, your mama went over to Flora to see a grave. She'd heard there was marker with a Woolsey under it."

"Was he there? Was it him?"

"Maybe. Who cares? He never left me anything to thank him for."

"Was his wife buried there, too? Tower says your grandma was a hooker."

"That old sonuvabitch." Ox's shoulders and spine straightened. His voice lowered. "You knocked his teeth in, didn't you?"

"No."

"You gotta teach 'em to respect you. That ain't respect."

"By hammering them? Yeah." Jiggs gave a sarcastic laugh. "Because that worked so well with me."

"If your life is so damn miserable, get on down the road."

"I have my accounts, you have yours. We live separate. The address just happens to be the same. If you'd keep your nose to *your* business, like you promised, then *my* affairs wouldn't bother you."

"My business is cattle, and our herds run together. What affects them, affects me."

"As I've said before, anytime you want to split off a section, we can run different ranches. I won't darken your door anymore."

"The only way this land will split is over my dead body." Ox stared.

"Good to know." Jiggs locked eyes with his dad.

Once every few months, they had a similar fight, different words, same reminders of the boundaries they'd cobbled together in earlier arguments. They both knew how it would turn out. Ox was stuck with Jiggs. He needed help and didn't trust hired hands. Jiggs had tried to leave once. Then Pax had died. Now guilt chained him to his older brother's place in the Woolsey family.

Ox looked away first. "Doesn't matter. You don't understand family pride. Forget it. I'll take care of Tower."

"No. You won't. I shouldn't have told you. No wonder you sit out here alone and don't have any friends."

Ox leaned back. He stared at his son for a moment then stood, pushing off the table for assistance. "People may not like me. They may cuss me. But they know I'm a hard worker. Anyone in three counties will tell you I keep my word. I don't cheat on a deal. They respect me and my family. I hope to God you can say that about yourself someday, 'cause it's lookin' slim."

Jiggs didn't reply. He watched Ox walk into the darkness, taking slow steps toward his house, his arms bent slightly from his sides, giving him balance.

With closed eyes, Jiggs let out a long breath and leaned back in his chair. Once again, he was the varmint son. The foul-up. And it was true; he'd thrown ice water over tonight's talk.

Ox's voice came from the darkness between their houses. "A long time ago, I told Tower he was so lazy he'd never wear out. He'd live his miserable life forever. And look...I was right."

"Yep. You were right." Jiggs got up, walked to the corner of the house, and watched until his father's door closed and the inside light blinked on.

He'd achieved his goals. He hadn't mentioned the skull and had discovered Bruno Woolsey probably wasn't buried in the creek. Big deal. In the process he'd hurt his dad, telling him he was friendless and his grandmother was a whore. All of it reminded his father that his favorite son was gone.

Jiggs still didn't know whose skull he'd stepped on, but it was becoming a rotted trap door to a dark past. Picking up his plate and table trash, he went inside. He had a phone call to make.

Don't Let the Bull...

THE NON-BURNED-out segments of the LED clock showed L:oo in the morning. Usually Jiggs woke up at that time, waiting for the phone to ring, but tonight, he hadn't gotten to sleep yet. Throwing back the covers, he slipped on a pair of moccasins and traipsed outside in his underwear. The night was quiet.

He paused by the corner of the house, looking for a light in the small cottage next door. All was dark. Walking quietly across the gravel, he wondered why a hard-nosed guy like his dad never seemed to have any trouble sleeping.

Slowly, he opened the door of the faded-blue pickup. He bent and twisted to get under the dash. In a minute he squirmed out and sat on the running board, stretching his back.

Crouching low, he pushed the door until it was almost closed. Then he nudged it with the palm of his hand, clicking it shut.

He turned and padded across the gravel, pausing at the corner of his house. All was quiet. All was dark—except for the stars watching from heaven.

*

The next morning Curly Dogs stood at the horse trailer. He snorted a couple of times, refusing to go in until he'd had the requisite amount of scratching between the ears.

"Wait up. I'll go up to Blank Map with you." Ox waved to Jiggs. His snap-button shirt was frayed at the cuffs. His jeans were raveled at the hems, but his boots, though worn, were waxed and well-tended.

"Not going to Blank Map." Jiggs led Curly Dogs into the trailer.

"Oh." Ox stuck his hands in his pockets and watched. "Where you headed off to?"

"I'm riding with Hop Hopkins."

"What's he got goin' on?"

"Don't know. He said if I wanted to talk, meet him over on the Shiny. Knowing Hop, it's a way to get work out of me."

"Don't go spreading family business around with that old buzzard." Ox gave Jiggs a withering look.

"Well, if you won't talk to me, I'll find someone who will. Or I'll discuss it with the sheriff if that's more to your liking."

"You're a piece of work. I'm asking you to shut up about the whole damn thing."

"I might if you'd tell me why. What's got you so riled? Whose skull is it? Family, stranger, enemy? How'd it get there?"

"It's a bad dream. Leave it. You think digging around will bring anybody back to life?"

"Tell me and I'll make up my own mind." Jiggs closed the trailer door and slid the bolt. "Oh wait. Everybody in this family has to think like you."

"It'd be a damn sight easier. Keeping you on point is like herdin' wasps."

"There are laws about finding bones." Jiggs stared at his dad.

"Let me tell you somethin'. Every man's trail is paved in bones. We all drag secrets behind us. If you live as long as me, you'll be freighted with more than your fair share. More than you're totin' now." Ox stared at him like a prospector assessing ore.

Jiggs felt he was on the receiving end of judgment day. There were plenty of things he'd kept from his dad. But he'd never told anybody the worst one. Ox looked as though he knew. He walked around his father and busied himself, checking the gear in the truck bed.

"You got time to ride with Hop, it'd be nice if you'd make time to ride fence with me one day. As I remember there were some good occasions in it. Nap should go too."

Jiggs was silent.

"Never mind." Ox walked away. "I'm busy anyway. Gotta get another part for that baler."

Jiggs looked up. "Don't go messing with Old Man Tower."

"Once a jackass, always a jackass."

"You talking about you or him?"

The cattle guard onto Shiny Creek Ranch made a vibrating *thump-thump-thump* as Jiggs drove over it. He passed through three more gates, wishing he had a teenager to hop out and open and close each one. It used to be his job when he rode with his dad. "Forty years later and it's *still* my job," he mumbled to the chickadee in the tree that had stopped chirping to watch him. A quarter-mile farther along a two-track path, he parked in a clearing beside a '70 Ford truck that had been top-of-the-line in its day. Now the side molding was falling off.

Dooley Munroe was hunkered by a rockjack, using a tire iron to twist two wires tight between fence posts. Jiggs' childhood buddy had aged, but was still lanky as though food refused stick to his bones. It was strange to see Hop sitting in a camp chair, near his horse, surveying Dooley's work. His broad-shouldered frame didn't carry as much weight as it used to. Both men watched Jiggs get out.

"This looks like an industrious outfit." Jiggs swung an open palm toward Dooley and had it met with a handshake.

"Something you wouldn't know fart about." Hop Hopkins stayed in his chair and reached out.

Jiggs gave his hand a single shake. "As I remember, Dooley, Sol, and I fixed this fence thirty years ago. Don't tell me it's falling down already."

"Yeah, I didn't get my money's worth outta you peahens." Hop slowly pushed to his feet. "You ready to ride? We'll check the rest of the fence."

Jiggs went back to his trailer and was tightening cinches when Dooley stepped beside him. "I don't know if this is such a good idea, but I couldn't talk him out of it. Here. Take this." Jiggs stared at the roped bundle he held out. "It's oxygen. Hop hates it. Won't carry it. But if he gets out of breath..." Dooley shook his head. "His nitro pills are in there, too."

"Good grief. Why didn't you call me? You think he's gonna die on me?"

"Some days, I think he could still toss you and me over a hay wagon. Other days, he has a hard time getting a breath."

"Maybe we oughtn't be doing this? You comin?"

Dooley shook his head. "Nope. He wants to talk to you, personal. He's set on it."

Jiggs took the bundle and threw several hitches over it, snugging it behind the saddle like a bedroll. He wore the face of a man who'd stepped into a water hole deeper than his boot tops. "I wanted to talk to him, not be the death of him. We won't go far."

As they walked toward the old man and his white quarter horse, Dooley's voice dropped lower. "He says he'll ride as long as he can sit a saddle, but if he's out for long, he'll be so sore, he won't be able to walk for a few days. Old age takes everybody prisoner."

"We don't have to ride. We can talk over there." Jiggs pointed to a stump.

Dooley didn't reply. He glanced at the old man who was standing ramrod straight and staring at him.

"I don't know what you're yappin' about," Hop said, watching Dooley take a step stool from the back of the Ford and set it next to the saddled horse. "But you look guilty as hell. Like that time you covered the sheriff's car in wet cotton balls and let 'em freeze overnight."

"Never proved it was me." Dooley looked at Jiggs. "Too bad it was such a long cold snap, huh?"

Hop kicked the step stool out of his way. "I don't need any hitch up. The day I can't get on a horse is the day I stop riding and shoot myself."

"The less you strain your heart, the better it'll be." Dooley held the bridle, in one hand and steadied the old man as he pulled himself into the saddle.

Jiggs threw a leg over Curly Dogs and looked at Dooley. "You gonna be here?" His former classmate nodded.

"C'mon, Jiggs." Hop reined Eagle and walked away. "When you two titsy-fritzels finish worrying, try to catch up."

Eagle had made the trip along the fence many times. He stepped over boulders and shouldered his way through sage brush.

"Maybe we shouldn't go too far?" Jiggs said.

Hop threw a look over his shoulder and reined Eagle sharply to the left, up a steep hill.

"Craphouse crickets," Jiggs mumbled as dirt clods and rocks bounced toward him. He pointed his horse's nose in the same direction. Curly Dogs snorted several times, letting Jiggs know he didn't think much of the off-trail excursion.

Topping the thirty-foot hill, they came into a flat meadow ringed with trees. A spring bubbled from a pool and ran to the downslope. Hop halted beneath a circle of pines, dropping the reins as he got off. Eagle lowered his head, cropping green shoots and spring flowers.

The old man wore an amused look. "After you called, I got to thinkin'. And I got a little matter I wanna talk to you about, too." He kicked around a boulder. Satisfied there weren't any snakes, he eased onto it and sat. "You go first."

"You need anything?" Jiggs asked.

"You wanna talk or nursemaid?" Hop waved him away. "Get on with it."

"I found something," Jiggs said quickly, looking at the old man for signs of fatigue. He still had the chiseled face, weathered and lean with hard work. The hair sticking out from under his cowboy hat was as white as it had always been. It didn't seem the old guy had changed much. Jiggs found a rock to sit on. "I was working Starvation Creek which has rerouted itself and left us dry. Anyway, I dug up a skull in the streambed. Real old. Everything has rotted. Just bone left."

"Dig a deeper hole and drop it back in." Hop gazed into the hazy purple distance.

"I'm pretty sure there's a law about that."

"When'd you start worryin' about the law? I remember you was always pullin' some empty-headed stunt. I had to vouch for you a couple of times."

"So why *did* you take me under your wing?"

Hop looked down and gently rubbed his eyelid with his thumbnail. "Ox took the passing of your mom pretty hard. Seemed like he had his own demons to fight without tryin' to raise you and Pax."

"You did the same for me when I lost Katie—arranging for Zinnia Roggs to take care of Nap. Then you worked me to death. I don't want to go through that again."

"That's what neighbors are for. Everybody goes through a hard spell. Now why's this old skull a problem? Throw it back in a hole and forget it."

"I figured the skull had a family. They might like to know where it ended up. If I turn it in, the authorities will get it where it needs to be. Yeah, I know," he cut off Hop who'd opened his mouth. "We'll lose money if they close of that land to dig. But Dad's acting like it's part of the Kennedy assassination. I think he knows whose skull it is."

"All the more reason to shut up." Hop took a breath, "Did you ever know Willy Springfield?" Jiggs shook his head. "The Springfields had been here a good while, prob'ly fifty years. Now that I think about it, this was before your time. Willy went to his graduation party in the granite quarry. Willy was talkin' and dancin' with a couple of girls. Bein' friendly and what not. He was the last person to see them alive. So they scooped up Willy and questioned him. The boy had been too drunk the night before to remember anything. People pointed fingers. The FBI got involved. When they couldn't find the girls, the authorities plowed up the Springfields' ranch, every acre of it, looking for those girls' bodies. Willy wasn't a bad kid. He'd knocked heads with the law several times, kinda like you." Hop gave Jiggs a measured look. "Well, long-story-short, Willy spent the next ten years, claiming he was innocent.

"Then we had a drought. Worse than now. Somebody walking the riverbed, found the back end of the girls' little Ford sticking out of silt and buckbrush. Those girls were still in it. No evidence of any foul play. They'd missed the corner and drove off, next to the bridge into the water. Even after the State apologized and let Willy out, tongues still wagged. His family sold out. Moved away from the stink that never shoulda been on their name."

"But that was a murder investigation. People were looking for their daughters."

"Yep. You don't know what you've got there, so you might have more government agencies involved. And heaven help you if it was a Nez Perce who died. You'd have the Department of Indian Affairs and an armload of tribal agencies involved. And for what? That skull could be anybody and come from anywhere. Probably from the plague year; it coulda washed into the crick and rolled downstream."

"Then why did Ox blow up when I told him about it? He went out and stomped it to pieces. He was mad. Not his usual you're-a-dumb-ass angry, but Armageddon fury. I don't know why he didn't take it and move it where I couldn't find it."

"Probably figured you'd tell somebody, and then they *would* dig up the whole ranch. Ox has his reasons to be pissed. You've only known him for forty-five years, but your dad lived a whole life before you showed up in this world. Hell, for that matter, we all did. I'd say he's had to freight a bigger load than most. Your granddad put him through hell."

"I've heard a few of the drinking stories."

"I remember the first time I saw Brick. I was a little shaver, sittin' on the corral fence."

"Was he drunk?"

"Far from it. You know how a kid looks when he hasn't grown into his man-body? They're dumb and clumsy, and you're pretty sure they're never gonna be any other way? Kinda like you." He didn't wait for Jiggs to answer, but continued, watching the breeze bend the yellow, thin-stemmed flowers. "Then the kid surprises you. Works hard and somehow goes from being a goosey-squirt to a man." He glanced at Jiggs. "Well, Brick wasn't that kid. He showed up at our corral, wearing a three-piece pinstripe suit, a Bowler hat, and shiny black shoes. He was a big-eared eastern tenderfoot. He introduced hisself and announced he'd come to work the Woolsey ranch. Opinion was, his mama had sent him back to Oregon to avoid going to France for the Great War."

76

"This was Bruno Woolsey's kid?" Jiggs asked. "The one he had by a saloon gal? Old Man Tower told me they'd become dignified and gone to Saint Louis."

"I don't recollect exactly where he came from or any stories about his mama. But his problem wasn't being a dandy. Dirt, boots, and time coulda put a cure to that. No, I'm sorry to tell you, he didn't have the common sense God gave a horse fly. I'm not talkin' about greenhorn screw ups. He'd make the same mistakes over and over. Part of his problem was that he trusted people. Or maybe he wanted folks to like him, so he'd go along with the crap they handed out.

"I got to see him a lot. He worked a deal with my dad. We could use his land for raising horses. He'd help break them, and they'd split the profits when they sold them to the army. The ranch hands were always putting him on the worst nag they had. I saw him try to mount a wrang that had froth foaming from its mouth. A fella named Totty Banks bet Brick that he couldn't ride it for thirty seconds. Totty was joshin', but Brick—he wasn't a loud man—he bit his bottom lip, assessing the whole affair, and mumbled. 'I can do it.'

"Totty had Brick out there, circling, looking for a way to step onto a nightmare. It took three men on ropes, holding that flipper down to keep it from heaving backwards. It was madder than a cut snake. My dad put the kibosh on the ride when he saw what was happening. He told him, 'If you die, I don't want to hunt up a new business partner.' 'Course, that was Brick's chance to get out with some dignity. Totty didn't razz him. He thought Brick would back out when he got near all the snortin' and flyin' dirt.

"Brick didn't seem to have a clue about the grace he'd been offered. He kept roundin' the horse and sayin', 'I can do this.'"

"Hard-headed." Jiggs nodded. "Sounds like a Woolsey."

"I guess he thought a manly act like that would snag him a reputation for being brave. And I suppose it was a courageous thing he was trying to do. But nobody saw it that way.

"I got off the corral fence and got down behind it. I could see Brick was scared. Hell, I was scared. The fellas holding the horse were scared. Brick barely got one foot in a stirrup when a volcano exploded in that very spot. Two of the men got drug before they could get free. Another flew in the air. As soon as they could, they were runnin'. Brick was glued to the dirt. I guess he didn't know enough to never let the bull between him and the fence."

Hop stared at the movie playing in air in front of him. "Brick stood, his hands out to his sides, watching that bronc jump straight in the air and then dive, planting all four hooves like he was trying to punch a hole through the earth. That horse's eyeballs were rolling in its sockets. On one orbit, an eye musta seen Brick, because the beast bounced like a pogo stick, straight for him.

"Men were yelling, 'Run!' 'Get outta there!' Brick stood like a dead tree, about as white-eyed as the horse." Hop shook his head. "I'll never forget it."

"Did he make the fence?"

"Nope." Hop smoothed one palm over the other. "That horse mowed right over him then turned to stomp him again. Totty jumped in, waving a blanket, and rodeo-clowned the nag to a side chute while a couple of other hands dragged Brick outta the corral.

"Broke his arm. I don't remember what else. He was sure proud of his 'bronc wounds.' I guess he thought it made him equal somehow to the boys getting wounded overseas or the ones breaking horses. I kinda felt sorry for him. He wanted to fit in, but didn't know how. He seemed to have a chink missing in his common sense. He suffered through some pretty mean jokes."

"You ever tell dad that story?"

"Hell no!" He looked as though Jiggs had suggested jumping off a cliff. "Ox would knock a kid's teeth down his throat if he said anything about a Woolsey. That was when we were younger. By the time we'd growed, we all had kin we didn't want to claim."

"If Brick was such an idiot, how did he marry and have kids?"

"I believe he kinda stumbled into a family. As I said, he was actually a tender-hearted guy. Violet Spinrad had a no-count jackass for a husband. I don't even remember his name. He'd take off mining and drinking and only return long enough to make another kid. They had five children and somehow she kept them all going. You talk about poor. They were probably eating vinegar pie and warm-water soup most of the time." Hop shook his head.

"Then the diphtheria rode over the territory. It took her young'uns in three days—all but the oldest. A five-year-old, named Lowell. I remember because he was the bravest kid, I'd ever knowed. Hell, he had more grit than most men. It was a terrible disease. It would waylay the littlest kids first. They'd say they didn't feel good in the morning and lay down. Gray, hairy fibers would grow through their noses and throats. Suffocate 'em. Nothin' anybody could do but watch it happen. They'd be dead by suppertime.

"Everybody was scared witless. My ma dusted the whole house with yellow sulfur and made us kids chew tobacco. She'd heard it helped. Maybe it did. It skipped over our ranch, but half the kids I knew were dead in a week. Some of the older folks, too."

Jiggs kept shaking his head, staring at the pine branches.

"You know, there's probably fifty kids buried in these hills." Hop pointed around him then his hand dropped to his lap. The silence played out for a long moment before he started again. "I hate to say this, and nobody would admit it, but most folks thought it was a blessing for Violet. She was workin' herself to death with all those kids. Now with just her and Lowell, she could go back to Mizzouri.

"Trouble was, she wouldn't leave. She'd settled a good piece of land. Said she'd lost too much to leave now. You know how those Spinrads are." Jiggs gave a sympathetic nod.

"Story goes that Brick married Violet to help her out. He was a soft touch like that."

"What about Violet's husband?"

Hop looked at the sky as though the history was written in the clouds. "I believe they found him dead at Opal's Sporting Club. But who knows if that's the truth? If something came up missing...socks, money, or a miner...everybody just said, 'It disappeared at Opal's.'"

"That's handy," Jiggs said.

"Yeah. It didn't help Brick, though. Anybody needed money, he'd lend it to them. Bamboozler, prospector, teacher needing school books—didn't matter who you were. He was too generous. Had to start selling land to pay his debts."

Jiggs lifted the side of his hat with his fingertips and scratched above his ear. "I suppose those were the homesteads Bruno Woolsey collected while he was rich. Are you trying to say my grandfather was a fool and my grandmother was a Spinrad? I heard yesterday my great-grandma was a saloon gal, I don't know how much more family history I can take."

Hop slapped him on the back. "Well, havin' a family of sinners and idiots is normal and human, but I can see why nobody would talk about havin' Spinrad blood. Those Spinrads think God created Adam and Eve, then He made them. They pop up everywhere, and they'll tell you they got there first. Buncha stiff-necked snobs. Truth is, my family and yours were here when this was nothing but sagebrush and bears rubbing themselves on pine trees. Used to be I could get on a horse and take off in any direction, never find a fence. Now, hell, the bears are almost gone. Axel Boley trapped and sold half of 'em to circuses. He'd kill a few, and sell the grease as a cure for..."

Jiggs let Hop's voice fade away. He'd heard the stories. What was new to him was his own family history. He wasn't pioneer stock. He'd come from a bunch of flunkies who'd gotten lucky a few times.

Wispy clouds stretched across the sky. The air at three thousand feet was cool and tinged with the scent of grass that would dry out in a month or so. Hop was rattling on about catching mountain goats. Jiggs had heard that story before, too.

He interrupted. "I can't believe I've lived here all this time and never heard any of this."

Hop looked at him. "Why would you? Who do you think you are?"

"I thought I was...from a pioneer family. Now I find out...Spinrads? For the love of Saint Pete."

"Oh get off your high horse. You're still a pup. If you last long enough to be an old fart like me...well, you don't have a clue yet of what goes on around here," Hop rasped. "You don't even know your own story, and you're fretting over one skull."

Don't Ask a Man His History

HOP HELD UP a hand. "I need to catch my breath. Air is thinner up here."

"Sure. sure." Jiggs leaned back on his boulder. "I'm thinking out loud here. I'm pretty sure the skull isn't Bruno Woolsey's. I hear he's buried in Flora, and his wife, my soiled-dove great grandma, is probably in a cemetery back east. That leaves the rest of my kin. I'm wondering what happened between Dad and Brick. Why's he hate him so much?"

Hop gave his head a single shake. "That's something Ox should tell you."

"Do you know?"

"You know the rules. Don't ask a man his history." Hop glanced sideways at Jiggs. "And never interfere with what ain't botherin' you." They sat for a while, listening to the water ripple down the hill. A couple of pine cones thudded to the ground, bouncing in the grass. "Forget what you dug up," Hop said quietly.

"I wish I could. It's not only about the skull anymore. Now it's turned into...good grief. I don't know what it is."

"Your history's always been there. You just didn't know about it. That don't change a thing, 'cept maybe take you down a peg."

"This is a little town. I can't believe nobody's told me anything."

"Since you wanted my advice and you're obviously not gonna take it, I'll say this once. Then we move on." He paused, looking at a lilac bush twenty feet away.

"Only a few old timers know history, and they don't give a damn. They got their own stories. The handful of us that's left are concentrating on drawin' our next breath. Nobody gives a shit if your gran-mama was Queen of England or queen of Opal's. Now c'mon."

He pushed off the boulder and walked to the bush. "This needs to be dug out again," he said as he kicked at the sides of a seep collecting a pool of clear water. He leaned over and smelled a purple bloom. "My grandma brought this over the Oregon Trail."

"Yes sir, you've told me," Jiggs said, hoping to the cut the story short. He'd heard a wheeze in Hop's voice.

"Years ago, I told you, I wanted to be buried over there." Hop pointed to a spot between the lilac and a pine tree. "I want you to make sure it happens. You do that?"

"Shouldn't you be telling Frank? He'll be the one in charge of the arrangements."

"I'm tellin' you. My son doesn't care about this place."

"He still building bridges in California?"

"Something like that," Hop mumbled, then quickly drew his hand to his mouth to cover a cough. "Damn." His voice was hoarse. "Been talking too much. I'm dry."

"I didn't bring water. Got oxygen."

"No." Hop pointed at the boulder in the shade, and Jiggs stayed next to him as he walked to it. "Don't get old," Hop said, leaning against the rock. "Go." He shooed his hand. "Mark my spot."

Jiggs found a branch, holding it vertical like a surveyor's pole. Hop waved him right and left. "There." Hop called. Jiggs tried to jam it into the ground. The hardpan was like stone. "I'll build a tripod. Rest there. You doin' okay?"

"Yeah. Yeah." The old man nodded.

Jiggs hurriedly gathered fallen branches. They'd pushed their outing too long already.

"Every time my great-gram went somewhere," Hop called, "she took a cutting from that bush."

"Save your breath. I'll be done in a minute," Jiggs yelled back.

"If she went to somebody's house, she always took a gift," Hop continued. "That's how you did it in those days."

Jiggs worked faster, leaning limbs against each other, tee-pee-style, as though building a fire. The old fart was as hard-headed as Ox. He'd keep talking until he fell over.

"Nobody had much back then." Hop pushed away from the boulder and rasped a low whistle. Eagle raised his head and walked toward Hop, stopping once to grab another bite of grass. Curly Dogs followed. "Granny would root a cutting. Get it started and gift it."

"We've got a lilac." Jiggs glanced up to see Hop fussing with the saddles. "It's a big old thing. Had it as long as I can remember."

"All the lilacs 'round here came from that bush." Hop continued checking cinches.

"There," Jiggs said, standing back to admire his work. He'd done a makeshift job. Most likely, deer, cows, or the wind would knock it over.

"What a pile of crap." Hop squinted at it. "I was screwin' with ya. Just make sure Frank plants me somewhere out here. And if you churn up one of my kin, don't go callin' the crime team."

Jiggs hesitated, unsure if he should help Hop mount. He knew the old cowboy would hate it. If it were his dad, Ox would have a heart attack from trying to beat Jiggs if he boosted him into the saddle. He stood close, pretending to check Curly Dogs' back hoof.

With a grunt, Hop mounted. "C'mon. Catch up," he said as Eagle walked off.

Jiggs and Curly Dogs trailed behind on the weedy wagon track. He was relieved they weren't sliding down the same slope they'd come up. The old man no longer sat as straight in the saddle. His body swayed side to side a bit. If he had a heart attack here, at least they could get a wagon in to haul him out.

A feeling of urgency pushed at Jiggs. He hated this, even though it was the same as every other foray into backwoods. There was always the threat of snake bite. A limb from a widowmaker could fall on them. Lightning strikes were common. Cougars stalked humans. The horse could stumble and roll over—or step in a hole. A thousand ways to die. And yet, a weak heart felt like a ticking time bomb.

Jiggs nudged Curly Dogs to ride beside Eagle. "You doin' okay?"

Hop nodded.

"I saw something I thought I'd never see," Jiggs said. "I was walking through the forest up at Blank Map, and in front of me a line of wild turkeys crossed the trail. I'd heard the Forest Service had introduced wild turkeys years ago."

Hop nodded again. Eagle plodded along at a steady, slow pace.

"I expected the turkeys to chatter a warning and take off, but instead they ran up the trail in front of me—toward a snake." Without turning his head, Jiggs saw Hop lean forward slightly. A readjustment in the saddle. That's all it was, he told himself. He continued telling his good story. A safe tale. Kinda humorous, mostly interesting. Far from the subject of a man not being what he once was. He was pretty sure both of them knew why he was filling the silence.

"So...the first turkey hen grabbed a rattlesnake about a foot long." Jiggs' hand waggled side to side. "She started flapping her head back and forth, drumming that snake on the ground. *Bang. Bang. Bang.* That's when the second turkey attacked her.

"The first bird jumped straight up the air and dropped the snake. The second turkey grabbed the rattler, and she pounded that snake's head in the dirt, too. When the poor rattler was finally dead, she threw him down, and they all they started pecking like a lunch buffet. Didn't eat all of him, though. Strangest thing I've ever seen."

Hop laughed as he re-seated himself in the saddle. The horses ambled along the weedy ruts. That was all Jiggs had in the way of funny stories. He began talking about Starvation Creek disappearing into the old lava bed.

Next to him, Hop stretched and resettled again. If the old guy hadn't been riding much, he was going to ache for several days. Obviously, the need to locate his gravesite must've been important if he was willing to suffer for it. Jiggs wondered if his dad was sore from sneaking out of the barn on Blue yesterday. Ox was probably rubbing his legs with horse liniment, but he'd never say anything.

As they rounded the bend in the road, Dooley hopped up from where he was sitting in the shade. "Tell Dooley that turkey story," Hop said as soon as they stopped.

"Where's the oxygen? Did you need it?" Dooley asked. Jiggs twisted in his saddle to unstrap the bundle, but it was gone.

Hop gave them a sly grin. "The damn thing musta disappeared at Opal's Sporting Parlor."

"You gotta stop ditching them. Home health services said they weren't gonna replace anymore. Someday you're gonna need it and you won't have it, you old buzzard." Dooley held Eagle's reins as Hop stepped down with a grunt.

"Quit your fussin'. You need to hear this story. Tell him, Jiggs." The old rancher sat in the camp chair.

"Is that why you had me running around in the pasture building stick forts? So you could dump your tank?" Jiggs stepped off Curly Dogs.

Hop smiled. "You know what to do when it's time."

Jiggs reached out his hand. "I'll help your son get you to the lilac bush."

Hop shook it. "Appreciate it."

Jiggs turned to Dooley, "I saw something I'd never seen before..."

He told the turkey story again. He added more gestures, and turkey sounds, taking them far from the niggling thought that one day, each of them might need an oxygen bottle.

Ox was bent over his partially finished bench, drilling holes in the seat for back braces.

"That's looking good," Jiggs said walking across the gravel drive. "Maybe you could make another one to put on Main Street. Grubbs Mercantile is the only place to sit."

"I'm glad you finally showed up." Ox held up an empty coffee can. "I swear I had some eight-penny nails, but they're gone. If you're gonna use something up, replace it. I can't get the truck started to go to town. I been banging around here, making do."

"What's wrong with your truck?"

"Hell if I know." Ox looked at the vehicle like it had betrayed him. "Won't even turn over."

"Typical Chevy." Jiggs said, walking toward the '79, its hood up, engine cavity exposed. "Battery dead?"

"I know enough to check a battery. It was *me* that taught *you* to work on engines, remember? There's nothing you can think of that I haven't tried."

Jiggs was prepared for this. He knew he'd have to take a load of insults to pull this off. He'd considered sneaking into his dad's house and hiding his keys. Ox would think he'd misplaced them but would never admit it. It would keep him from driving for a few days. Help him simmer down about Old Man Tower.

Then again, it was doubtful such a ploy would stymy him. He'd simply jam a screwdriver into the ignition to turn the switch.

On Jiggs' early morning foray, he'd cut the main power wire going into the Chevy's fuse box. If Ox found it, there'd be the devil to pay, but Jiggs doubted his dad could kink up enough to get under the dash to look.

It was a crappy thing to do. He should've felt worse, but he didn't. Guilt was a small price to pay for the peace of mind he'd had today. Ox wasn't a man to make puffed up threats. He'd consider it his duty to drive to Two Pan and give Old Man Tower a lesson in keeping his mouth shut.

Ox leaned over the engine, checking the distributor cap. "I switched this battery with the tractor battery. Everything works fine. Both of them are charged. The fuses look good. It's like the thing went kerflooey for no reason."

"You want me to tow you to Slat's?"

"Hell no. That grease monkey knows less about an engine than you do."

Jiggs kept his head down and his smile to himself. Ox would rather walk than pay someone for mechanic work.

"New starter?"

"Maybe." Ox scowled at his faded-blue vehicle.

"How about dinner at the Bar and Grill? We'll stop by Grubbs and order your part. Then drop off a check at the feed store. Tracy says we owe for last month."

"Like hell we do. I paid that in person." Ox put his drill into his wooden tool box.

Jiggs closed the Chevy's hood. "If your truck is on the fritz, when'd you drop it off? 'Cause she told me yesterday."

"I pay my bills on time. Always have. She doesn't know where she put it. She's always yakking like a chickadee when I go in. Wears me out to hear her go at it. One more damn thing *I* have to sort out. No water in the creek. No nails. Broken down truck..." He was still mumbling and cussing as he toted the tool box to the garage.

Jiggs smiled and shook his head. He shouldn't be enjoying this. Like a hot wind, Ox would change directions and blow over him soon, but for the moment, it was good to let the disloyal truck take the heat.

Neither man spoke on the drive to town. It had taken years for Jiggs to cultivate the silence. As a teenager he'd ridden, staring out the window, ignoring his dad's judgments on who'd done a crappy job putting up a fence, or why Charlie Coldwell was a sorry pick for county commissioner. When Pax was alive, they'd quietly elbow each other until their game got rowdy enough for Ox to smack both of them across their heads. Pax always got the shotgun seat next to the window, so Jiggs got more of the blow.

After Pax died, celebrating his twentieth birthday, it was Jiggs, his dad, and silence in the truck. They'd kept it that way for twenty-eight years.

Jiggs drove through town and parked at the south end of Main Street in front of a red barn-like building. "Grubbs Mercantile" was painted in fat white cursive letters across the side. A red-haired, ragged-eared dog sat on a bench beside the door. It didn't look up, but kept licking its butt as the two men got out of the truck.

"Get offa there." Ox hissed, holding onto the backrest and nudging the hound from the seat with his boot.

"You better hope folks don't treat you like that just 'cause you get old." Jiggs held the screen door open for his dad.

"If I start licking my butt in public, you've got permission to shoot me."

"Good to know."

"We Boil at Different Degrees"

—Ralph Waldo Emerson

THE FAMILIAR PUNGENT scent of oiled oak floors greeted Jiggs and Ox as they walked into Grubbs Mercantile. Somewhere between the narrow aisles stacked high with merchandise was anything a person needed—if he or she had patience to search for it.

Augustus Grubbs had rolled his wagon into the Eagle Caps right behind the miners of 1860 and hawked salt, flour, beans and britches. When fires wiped the town off the map, he'd reconstructed his building—until 1920—when folks decided there were better places to be. Places with cars and street lights. That was the last time the old two-story structure had been updated, except to add electricity.

Fluorescent lights hung from the high ceiling, next to brass-brimmed coal-oil lamps. White-enameled deli cases displayed cold cuts and home-grown hamburger. A deer's head with a broken antler hung high on a wall between boxes of boots which were retrieved via a rolling ladder. The glass-front oak display cases showed off earphones for an iPod, piled on top of ropes and riding gloves. There used to be an electric register, but Cleova Klegg, the checker, preferred to use the massive black till that made a *ding* when the drawer opened. She said there was something more satisfying about hearing your money being spent.

"I been wanting some marshmallow crème to snack on," Ox said to the stock boy stuffing boxes of BBs under a shelf. "Where do you hide it?"

The sixteen-year-old looked as if he'd been asked the square root of pi. "I dunno. Do we carry it?"

Grumbling, Ox stomped off, the old floor boards creaking under his feet. Jiggs found Andy Grubbs in the back of the store, sitting in one of the armchairs, solving the world's problems with a few townsfolk.

"Hey Andy, I need to order a part," Jiggs said to the proprietor then headed to the side room crowded with fan belts, sparkplugs, and car manuals hanging by strings from the walls.

For a round-bodied, plump-faced fellow, Andy Grubbs moved surprisingly quickly. He sprang out of the chair, removing the pencil he kept behind his ear. "Now what is it you need? Maybe I've got it in stock?"

When they were out of earshot of the others, Jiggs said quietly, "I don't actually need a part. I'm just letting Dad think I'm ordering it. It's for his truck."

"Oh. I see." The shopkeeper nodded, one eyebrow arched. "You want to know how much the part you're not ordering costs? You know he'll ask."

"Yeah. That's a good idea. Make it expensive," Jiggs said.

Andy pinched his lip between his fingers and thought a moment. "I don't think so. He'll bad mouth me all over town, and Slats GasNGo is having a half-price sale on Armor All and strut installation. No need to convince any customers to go to him."

"All right. It doesn't matter what you charge for this part that I'm not ordering. But tell him it won't get here for a couple of weeks."

"I see." He continued pulling his lip. "Well, really, I don't understand, but when it comes to your dad, I don't ask questions. Problem is...he'll cuss me about the delay, too. He's my worst advertiser."

"Okay. Make it cheap enough he's willing to wait for it."

"How about I tell him I may be able to get one for free?"

"He'll still—"

"I'm not an employee here!" Ox's voice boomed from the front of the store.

Andy Grubb pushed past Jiggs and a barrel holding windshield wipers. "What seems to be the problem, Mr. Woolsey?" he called as he hurried up the aisle. Jiggs was right behind him. They found Jason, the stock boy, cowering at the till with Ox staring him down.

"Since your hired hand hides all the stock around here..." Ox shook a plastic canister at the boy. "I figured he could tell me where he buried the marshmallow crème. But he seems surprised that this is a grocery store and asked me if Grubbs carried it. So I went digging through shelves..."

Andy Grubbs closed his eyes and let out a sigh.

"I finally found it. On a bottom rack, stuffed behind bags of marshmallows. I brought it up here to pay, and the kid says..." Ox glowered at the young man, who was staring and running his finger across the till's metal scrollwork. "The kid says, 'Hey. You found it. Where was it?' I told him he could find it himself."

"I'm sorry, Mr. Woolsey." Andy turned to Jason. "I'll take care of this. You go fix the cooking aisle." The boy quickly took off.

"You know how long I've been coming here, giving you business?" Ox set the canister at the checkout.

"Dad..." Jiggs' voice carried a warning.

Ox narrowed his stare at Andy Grubbs. "You'd think somebody would say, 'Hello, Mr. Woolsey' or 'Good to see you again' when I come in. But, no. I'm a nameless old geezer. 'Buy somethin' or move along.' Customers are treated like they're invisible here. Millie walked in a minute ago." He waved toward a fuzzy-haired woman. Her gold-rimmed glasses sat crooked on her nose. "Nobody said, 'Hi' 'Whadda ya need?' or even 'Go to hell, Millie.'" The woman nodded.

"Dad..." Jiggs said again, but Andy held up his hand.

"I apologize, sir." A pink flush was climbing his neck. The edges of his ears had turned red. He took a breath and let it out. "I assure you that you are important to us. I'll talk to Jason right now." He turned and walked away.

"Dad it's like you rain down a crap-storm wherever you go."

"That's why I don't go out much. Nobody's got the common decency to talk anymore. It's all about 'gimme your money.' Look." He held up the marshmallow crème. "I'm standing here with my wallet open and nobody cares. Not a soul around to take my money. It's a damn miracle they've stayed in business."

Jason jogged to the front of the store and stepped behind the till. "Sorry to make you wait, Mr. Woolsey. I was putting the marshmallow bags back from where you'd scattered them on the floor. Sorry to make you look for this. I should've helped you. I'm glad you found what you needed, Mr. Woolsey. That'll be three dollars and fifteen cents, please, sir."

Ox scowled at the boy. He pulled bills out of his wallet one at a time, placing them on the counter. Andy stood nearby, observing and helping Millie free one of the tiny shopping carts nesting inside the next one.

Jason popped open a paper sack. "Would you like me to bag that for you, Mr. Woolsey?" Ox nodded.

The boy dropped the small canister in the big sack and held it out. "And how are you feeling today, sir? You doin' all right?"

"None of your damn business. Why the hell would you care?" Ox snatched the sack, eyeing the boy up and down.

"Dad, why don't you go over to the Bar and Grill and get us a seat?"

"Why? You think they're gonna run out of chairs suddenly?" Ox switched his gaze to Andy who was moving packages of cookies to "face out" the shelves. "You got my truck part?"

"It'll take about a week, sir." Andy said, noticing Jiggs shaking his head behind Ox. "Well...maybe more. I'm trying to get one for you for free."

"Free?" Ox squinted. "You can't trust free. Nothing you get for free ever works. Order a Chevy relay and have 'em ship it to the house."

"You could get your grandson to do that on the internet for you, sir," Jason said. "It's quick and easy—" He stopped, seeing Jiggs violently shake his head. "Oh! Sorry, sir. That's just foreign models that have internet parts. You don't drive a rice rocket, do you sir?"

Ox looked at the boy as though he were a bag of talking hair.

"Say," Jiggs' tone was light, announcing a change in the subject. "Since the Grubbs have been here as long as the Woolseys, what do you know about our early days?" he asked Andy.

The proprietor straightened cans of insect repellant. "I was told one of your kin took off with Grubbs Mercantile."

"That'd be a trick. What'd he do with it?"

"Bruno Woolsey moved it, along with his establishment, to this spot. My great-granddad helped." His eyes flitted toward Ox then at the floor. "I think Bruno had uh...an entertainment house."

"Saloon." Ox wore a silencing stare.

"Okay, I see. And across the street, my relatives had the mercantile. This was the time they had sunset laws."

"Oh...yeah." Jason wagged his finger. "I heard about that in history class. The Chinamen, who worked the mines, couldn't be above ground after sunset."

"So they dug tunnels to live in and to go from store to store. That way they could get food and supplies after dark. Story goes, they dug a big tunnel between the mercantile and the...saloon across the road. So big, it fell in one day, along with a horse and rider going down the street. The horse was standing in a ditch with the rider's eyeballs even with the surrounding road."

"How'd they get the horse out?" Jason asked.

"They didn't. They shot him and filled in the tunnel."

"That's bullshit," Ox said. "Who told you that story? Nobody would kill a good horse. They dug a ramp and walked him out." Jiggs gave his dad a surprised look.

"Well, however they fixed the mess," Andy continued, "it left a mound in the middle of the street. You know you can't fill in a big gap like that. It either sinks and collects water or humps and jolts the wagons as they cross. So that winter, after everything had iced over and the thermometer hadn't peeked above zero for a week, Bruno Woolsey hooked teams of horses onto his sporting palace and dragged it across the frozen ground to a flat place. Pretty soon the whole town had been skidded a quarter mile south, to this very spot."

Ox scowled. "Those buildings would've come apart at the joints."

"That makes him Two Pan's first 'mover and shaker.'" Jason grinned, then noticed Ox's glare and added, "Sir."

"What a buncha hogwash." Ox turned and left.

"What's eating him?" Jason rolled his eyes. "He's grumpier than usual."

Andy Grubb looked at the boy and pointed to a stack of cardboard boxes. Jason shrugged, cut open a carton, and started hanging jerky sticks.

"Sorry." Jiggs motioned for Andy to walk outside with him. "Dad's been in more of a twist than usual, lately. I've been digging into family history."

"Well, we all boil at different degrees." Andy tucked his pencil behind his ear. "I heard you found a gold watch on your place. Are you trying to figure out who it belongs to? They say the initials on the fob aren't legible."

Jiggs hesitated, collecting his words. Good thing he hadn't told the truth and said he'd found a skull, the news would've traveled even faster. As it was, the watch story had picked up added details. Creech Walters must've asked a few people in an attempt to help out. After all, what would be secretive about finding a watch? "I'm thinking it may belong to some of my early kin. You've been around a long time. As I said before, do you know any stories about the Woolseys?"

"I once saw your dad throw a fella into a truck bed then heave a block of ice on top of him. But don't tell Ox I said that." Andy glanced over his shoulder. "That was years ago when we had the ice locker out back. Some guy made a rude comment about your mom."

"I'm surprised she didn't take a horsewhip to the guy. She could take care of herself," Jiggs said. "Who was it?"

"Somebody passin' through. Everybody around here knows that Ox doesn't brook any talk about his family." He glanced at Jiggs. "Unless he's the one doin' it."

"Yeah. Yeah." Jiggs looked away. "I meant earlier stories. You ever heard anything about my granddad, Brick?"

"I don't gossip." Andy shook his head. "Folks may sit around the stove in my store and tell stories, but I don't spread them."

"Ox isn't going to find out," Jiggs said as he waved at Lottie and Zim Lubach driving past.

Andy bit his lip. "I overheard my granddad say something, but I've never repeated it. I swear." He held up his hand as though giving testimony. "The dentist..." he pointed at a narrow second-story window above the store. "You know how he up and disappeared, a hundred years ago. Left everything lying there?" Jiggs nodded.

"Well, there'd been a bank robbery and a shootout in Enterprise a couple days before. My granddad believed the robbers holed up at Brick's ranch and sent him to fetch the closest thing we had to a doctor."

"Are you saying my granddad was part of a gang?"

"No. No." Andy waved his hands. "My granddad suspected that Brick took in the wounded robbers. Especially if they threatened his wife or kids."

"Why Brick?"

"Granddad saw him in town late at night and thought it was strange. It's far-fetched, I know. That's why I've never said a word, even though the dentist is the topic of discussion every day. People come in each morning to see if his ghost has moved stuff around during the night."

"I bet that's good for business." Jiggs gave him a flat stare. "All right. So why would outlaws let Brick go, but not the dentist? Usually, they paid a doc and turned him loose so he could patch them up another day."

Andy shrugged. "Only Brick knows."

"Now wait a minute." Jiggs leaned forward.

"Sorry. My granddad thought that Brick Woolsey was the reason this town lost its only medicine man. You asked. I told you. No need to get mad. I thought the watch you found might've been one of the bank robbers'—or the dentist's."

Jiggs let out a long breath, aware Andy was watching him. His list of skull suspects had ballooned to include Violet Spinrad's missing husband, a tooth puller, and a gang of bank robbers. Each story he'd heard had made his ancestors into rounders, laggards, and idiots.

If he kept looking into his family, he'd probably find gun runners and slavers, too. Maybe Ox wasn't as cantankerous as he'd thought; his old man was simply tired of hearing the stories. Thrashing everyone who repeated them didn't seem so ridiculous anymore.

"Sorry. You're right. I did ask." Jiggs gave Andy a nod. "Well, maybe that's why the ghost comes back and moves things around. He's looking for the truth, too. I hope he's had better luck finding it than I've had."

If You Can't Fix it With Duct Tape, You Haven't Used Enough

JIGGS WALKED INTO the Bar and Grill. He had great hopes for "burrito night." His previous strategy to skirt around the subject of the skull had failed. He wasn't good at it like his mother had been. She could pierce a person with a perceptive look or a smooth-sounding, "If that's what you think." She'd let her unspoken questions circle and hover like a storm, building in the distance, rolling nearer and nearer, until it was a relief to confess and get the lightning strikes over.

Tonight, Jiggs had a different plan. Ox was usually in the mood to talk after a good meal. He liked to tell stories. With luck, Jiggs could get a piece of the puzzle answered.

A few Two Pan residents were scattered in the dining area. Several waved as he walked in. The *clack* of pool balls came from the side room. His usual spot was taken by a family from Minam, celebrating a birthday. A cake sat at Table 2, and gift-wrapped packages lay under their chairs as a pinched-mouth woman asked Misty for more chips and salsa.

In the corner, a man the size of a small building beckoned Jiggs toward him. Because of his weight, George Jugenmeir was relegated to Table 4. As a former logger, he'd been a hefty man, but years of eating lumberjack breakfasts long after he'd quit bucking timber had tripled George to "hulk" size. After breaking several chairs, Bazz had reinforced the seats at Table 4 so they'd support the man's mass when he came to eat.

"Take a load off, neighbor." George waved a thick hand.

"Hey. How ya doin'? I'm scouting for Dad. He been in here?"

George swung his heavy head back and forth. "Join me and wait. Seems we don't talk over the fence anymore."

"Be glad to, but first I need to find him. He's already chewed up a stock boy. No telling—"

"I saw him." Chicken Thief Bob skidded to a stop beside the table. "He's down the street, sitting on a bale of sawdust, talking to Tracy." The skinny man had a handle on most things happening in the area. Born in Two Pan, he chose to stay and drive a gravel truck for a living. His jeans hung loose from his waist, as though his belt were the only thing keeping them up. His shirt sleeve flapped as he snapped his fingers. "Hey! You figured out who the watch belongs to yet?"

Jiggs blinked. "Sometimes I forget how fast news travels. Well..." he hesitated, looking for words. "I figure it belongs to me. I found it." He hoped that would put a stop to the tale.

"I heard Lottie Lubach can't find her old watch. Have you looked inside? Is there a picture of her grandma in there?"

"What I found was broken up," Jiggs said, thinking of the skull. "Doesn't have a face."

"I'll go tell her." He pointed to the back room used for meetings. "I got roped into helping the Daughters of Two Pan plan the Fourth of July shindig."

"Lucky you." Jiggs shooed him away. "Don't mention our names."

As he walked off, Misty sat beers in front of Jiggs and George. "We're getting busy. Order now. I'm not coming back two or three times to see if you're ready."

Jiggs ordered burritos for Ox and himself. George requested three. They watched the twenty-two-year-old blonde turn and extort an order out of the next table. George said, "You know whose watch it coulda been?"

Jiggs took a drink. Next thing he knew, someone would call a TV station about the trumped-up timepiece.

"There used to be a shack on that strip of land. More like a chicken house, really."

"Owned by Abraham Spinrad." Jiggs swiped the foam from his lips with the palm of his hand. "I went to county records. Looked it up."

"Yeah, but ol' Abe let one of his daughters and her lazy husband live there."

"Cal Mosley," Jiggs said. "Dad told me about that."

"It's doubtful the watch was theirs. They didn't have two beans to rub together, but it could be from some of the Spinrad clan. When the Spinrad gal finally moved off the place, your dad bought it before I could. Nice little piece of land. Stream running through it. He tore down the camp-house and dammed up the ditches so water continued down the creek to his and my properties. I always wanted that parcel." He let out a sigh. "It wouldn't do me any good now, though. If it is a Spinrad watch, keep it. It'll be the only thing you'll ever get out of them."

"How you doin' tonight?" Ox interrupted as he dragged a heavy chair out from the table and sat down.

"Worse now that you're here to catch all my lies." George raised his beer to Ox.

"I ordered you a burrito—steak," Jiggs told his father. "Get your own drink, if you can catch her. Did you get Tracy paid up?"

"I told you, I paid her last week." Ox's voice was thorny. "I was down there listening to her jabber. That woman can talk."

"You enjoyed it." George elbowed him. "Since my Vetta's been gone and the kids have moved away, the only gal I get to talk to is Misty here."

The waitress smiled as she slid oval plates of burritos and mole sauce onto the table. "And the only conversation you get out of me is, 'Here's your dinner.' You need anything else?"

"A lemonade," Ox said, and then he proceeded to tell George his plan—which included explosives—to fix the dried-up creek. Then he cussed the uselessness of the town donkey. Jiggs bedeviled him about the neddy and the dynamite to keep him distracted. He didn't want the conversation to lull and George mention the imaginary watch again. A sudden thought made Jiggs pause. It seemed there was a lot of deception in his dealings with his dad: a truck starter that was never ordered, a watch that never existed, ear chips hidden in cattle, and the lies he'd covered up since he was a teenager.

He decided he'd have less guilt if he steered the conversation toward George. "What are your kids doing now?"

"My boy's fixing computers in Oregon City. My daughter is supporting her stupid husband. He quit his government job in California to become a writer. He's typing his memoirs." George took a drink then decided he needed another and gulped a long swig. "He's only thirty. He hasn't lived long enough to do anything interesting except run over a few snakes with the county road grader. All of 'em say they're not coming back here. My bunch couldn't give a damn. You're lucky, Ox. You've got Jiggs to carry on what you started."

Ox pushed his empty plate away. "I've never had a boo-rito before. Not bad. Order some lemon pie for dessert. I gotta find a bathroom."

George frowned at Ox's back disappearing down the dark hallway.

"The wrong son will inherit his empire." Jiggs shrugged and signaled Misty. "He doesn't like to talk about it."

The men were silent, watching the birthday boy tear paper off a present. The fourteen-year-old pulled a pair of chaps and a roll of duct tape from the box. Surrounding tables laughed and applauded the items symbolizing his rite of passage. Every man believed in the miracle of duct tape. It was the first gadget to go into his manhood toolkit. The boy stood and held the long chaps to his legs. A red T.K.C., his initials, was tooled into the leather on each leg.

"I remember my first pair." Jiggs shook his head. "When the straps broke, I wore Pax's. He wasn't going to use them ever again. I thought Dad was going to come unglued."

"Ox has been hard on you since the truck crash, but he'll mellow out. We all do."

"Good grief, George. It's been over twenty-five years."

"It'll take Ox longer because of his dad."

"What do you know of Brick? You have any idea how he died or where he's buried?" Jiggs pointed to 'Lemon Pie' on the menu as Misty walked by. She nodded.

"He was a sweet ol' fellow. Drunk or sober. It was a damn shame how he ended up." George shook his head.

"Jiggs!" Chicken Thief Bob called as he ran to the table. "Ox fell in the bathroom." Jiggs stood, not hearing the rest of what Bob was saying.

"I didn't fall! Quit your squealing," Ox yelled, walking slowly down the dark hallway. "Buncha damn Taiwanese-made junk." He waved an empty toilet roll holder in his fist. The screws protruded from the metal dispenser. A hunk of sheetrock hung on one corner. "Damn shoddy work. Popped off. Right in my hand."

"You okay?" Jiggs crossed the room.

"Hell yes." Ox shook his arm free of his son's hand. "Let's get outta here." He looked at the people who were watching him. "Be damn happy it didn't happen to you," he announced. "An outhouse would be better than that booby-trapped crapper back there." He tossed the dispenser as he went out the door. It clattered across the bar and onto the floor.

"Misty," Jiggs called. "Could I get my bill?"

"I'll stay with him." Chicken Thief looked at the door then Jiggs. "I was waiting to use the restroom when I heard a commotion. I went right in. He seems okay. I think he was mostly embarrassed to be caught with his pants down. He didn't start cussing 'til I got him up."

"He'll tolerate you, better than me. He'll rip me up if I try to look him over right now." Jiggs said to Chicken Thief. "I'll check the damage and pay the bill."

"Yeah, yeah. He seems his normal self." The skinny man nodded. "He's already cussed me out. I'm immune, now."

Jiggs stepped into the bathroom. A ragged hole gaped from the sheetrock where the toilet roll dispenser had been. A sign stating, "Put the lid down when you finish" lay on the floor. The trash basket was overturned. He flushed the remains in the toilet and used the side of his boot to sweep pieces of sheet rock into a corner.

"Looks like he used the dispenser as a support bar," Bazz said, leaning through the door. "Used it to push up. Came off in his hand."

"Sorry about this. I'll come by to fix it tomorrow."

"I was in the kitchen. Heard the noise. Don't worry about it. I need to put one of those assist bars in here anyway," Bazz said. "If you can't blow a bathroom out on burrito night, it's probably not very good Mexican food."

"Thanks." Jiggs nodded. "I'll be by tomorrow." When he passed through the dining area, conversations had resumed. A few women nodded, wearing the sympathetic face they saved for young women herding cranky toddlers.

Misty picked up empty mugs, telling him, "You go on. George got your ticket."

He called across the bar, "George, I owe you." The big man shook his head, and Jiggs headed for the door.

Outside, Ox sat on the passenger side of the truck, staring straight ahead. The door was open and Chicken Thief Bob was rattling on about Dooley Monroe getting chewed out for using his metal detector under the football stands.

Jiggs recognized the story—not that he'd heard it before—but it had the same tone and lightness he'd used to distract Hop from his thoughts. Deception. They all dealt in smoke and mirrors instead of putting words out in the open. He noted it was a good thing that Chicken Thief had his foot on the running board; otherwise, Ox might've shut the door on him.

"Jiggs?" a woman called. Tracy's dark hair bobbed as she hurried down the street, carrying a plastic container with a couple pieces of pie inside. "Here. I heard." She pushed it in his hands, staring past him at Ox. "I think he needs this. He's had a hard week."

"Thanks. Did you get paid for the feed?"

She nodded. "He wrote me a check tonight." She followed him to the truck, reaching, past Chicken Thief to pat Ox's arm.

Jiggs got in, listening to them make a few jokes before they shut the pickup door.

As he drove, he glanced at his dad. He'd planned on the meal softening up Ox. A relaxing, enjoyable evening. His father's hard, angular face was outlined by the dashboard lights. Ox's jaw was clenched. His eyes shiny.

Lemon pie rode between them.

Jiggs didn't speak. It was the only way he knew to love the unlovable.

In Dog Years, I'm Dead

THE FOLLOWING MORNING Jiggs knocked at Ox's door, holding the lemon pie. There was no answer. The door creaked as he opened it and stuck his head inside. "Dad! You up yet?" The house was quiet. Jiggs stepped into the combo living-dining room.

Ox had never been a tidy housekeeper, but the place looked like a hermit's dump. Stacks of newspapers leaned against the furniture. Paper plates with dried sandwich crusts sat on top of mounds of clothes. In the kitchen, the cabinet tops were cluttered with cans of nails, tools, and coffee mugs. Five peanut butter jars filled with water sat in the sink. Oil and particles floated on the liquid's surface.

When Jiggs' mother had died, Ox had assigned the boys chores. He'd whip his belt off and pop it across the back of their jeans if they fought about who did what. Their home had been passable for bachelor living.

The sound of a dropping boot came from the bedroom. Jiggs walked by the alcove with its old roll top desk. The ledger book for the ranch was open and lying on top. A pile of black licorice gumdrops and a mound of almonds sat on the green-lined page. He frowned, remembering the time he'd been strapped for leafing through the book, deciding for himself if there was enough spare money for the horse he'd wanted.

The creak of the bed made him hurry toward the back of the house. He rounded the door and came face to face with his dad.

"What the hell are you sneakin' around about?" Ox ran his hand across the front of his shirt.

"Did you sleep in that?" Jiggs pointed. Ox pushed past him and headed for the kitchen. "Are you just now getting up, Dad?"

"Why the hell are you here?" Ox opened the fridge door partway and stared inside.

"I brought this. Tracy sent it last night, but you were too ticked off to hear me." He held out the clear plastic box of lemon pastry.

Ox took it, opened a drawer, looked in, and then shoved it shut. He grabbed a fork from a dirty plate on the counter.

"When did you start living like this?" Jiggs squinted and looked around.

"Always." Ox stuffed a forkful of lemon custard in his mouth. "You never noticed. Why should I put on party airs? Nobody comes to visit. What are you doin' here?"

"I came to see if you're all right." Jiggs picked up *Cattle and Ranch* magazines from a kitchen chair and tossed them on the table as he sat down. Several sealed envelopes skittered from the pages. "This is the feed bill." Jiggs picked one up. "And this is—"

"Just put it right back where you found it." Ox's voice carried a threat.

"But..."

"I know damn well what it is, and that's where I want it. Put it back." He waved the fork at Jiggs and gave him a hot stare until Jiggs slid each envelope back into the pages of the magazine.

"Are you going to pay those bills?"

"They've already been paid. That's why they're there. Don't worry about it."

Jiggs scrutinized his father. "Are you gonna be able to get around today?"

"Hell no. My pickup's broke."

"I meant..." He paused a few seconds, letting Ox's voltage frizzle from the air. "Are you sore? Do you need liniment? Maybe a doctor?"

"No." Ox focused on his pie. "I got BenGay."

"I can tell." Jiggs waved a hand past his nose as he got up. "How're you fixed for groceries?" He opened the fridge to find half a loaf of bread, a re-sealable package of wrinkled bologna, and an open jar of marshmallow crème with a spoon sticking out of it. "Dang. You're out of peanut butter, huh? Breakfast of champions. Why didn't you get it last night?"

"Buncha birdbrains working at Grubbs. I'm not giving him money. I'm shopping over at Minam from now on."

"Okay." Jiggs braced both hands on the counter, leaning into it. "That'll put Grubbs out of business for sure. I'm going to..."

He'd stopped talking for two reasons. He was headed to town to fix the hole Ox had ripped in the bar's restroom. His second thought was that it would be better not to mention last night. As he pushed off the counter, one hand stuck. "Jeez Louise, Dad. Is this jelly?"

"Outta that, too."

"Okay. Tonight Nap and I are going clean up this stable. If you don't want us helping, then you'd better get snapping and tidy up."

"I've got a bench to build."

Jiggs paused at the door. "I thought you were out of nails. I didn't see you buy any last night when we were at Grubbs."

"Shit. Now I'll have to sit around 'til you bring some." He grunted slightly as he lowered into a recliner and flipped out the leg rest. "Seems like I've been waiting on you for something my whole life."

Jiggs went out the door, reminding himself not to slam it. He remembered the whipping Ox had striped across his backside once before for flinging a door shut and breaking the glass.

"Are you up there, Pop?" Nap called.

"Yep." Jiggs leaned on a pitchfork, staring through the outer doors used to load hay into the loft. He watched Harriet, the dried-up, black and white milk cow, repeatedly try to stick her head into a pile of gopher dirt like she was an ostrich.

He should have gone to town, but for reasons he wasn't quite sure of, he had climbed to the loft instead. He'd spent a lot of time there as a kid.

Nap's well-worn straw hat rose up the ladder until the young man stepped into the loft. "You don't have to do that. I was gonna scrape up the broken bales."

"It's okay. I've always liked the view." Jiggs turned back to stare out the loft doors. Black Angus ate bunch grass. Harriet chased a piece of paper blowing across the field. "I can't wait to get rid of that weird bag of bones. She thinks she's a dog."

"Why does Gramps keep her? She doesn't produce."

"She makes him laugh."

"Well, I guess that's worth something." Nap stood beside him, focused on the same vista. "Everything okay?"

"Something's screwy with your granddad." Jiggs recounted the incidents of the toilet roll holder and the unopened bills in the magazine. "I told Ox that you and I would clean up his place tonight."

"Oh hell, that'll be frickin' World War III."

"You know, your mother or I didn't cuss like that. Where 'd you pick that up?"

"Granddad. He gave me the vocabulary to get through college. Bless his soul."

"Never mind." Jiggs used the pitchfork tines to scrape hay into a pile. "Back your truck up to his door by six. He's got a lot of newspapers to haul off. Don't toss anything without looking through it. But don't let him know we're checking for mail. Or money."

"You know normal families get together and toss a baseball around."

"The only thing I've ever seen him hurl was a hoe. Right over my head. I may have deserved it that time. I left a gate open. The calves got into my mom's garden."

"But you played baseball." Nap picked up the broom hanging from a stud and began sweeping. "Who taught you?"

"Hop Hopkins. And I had a brother to play catch with. Is that what this is about? You wanna play baseball?"

"I came up here because I wanted to talk to you about a bull. It's time we stepped up to genetically-engineered breeding stock. It'll improve the herd, and we can get better prices. I've worked up the costs and projected gains if you'll listen."

"The timing is poor. The only asset I know that's on the ranch ledger right now is licorice drops and almonds. Help me 'black op' your granddad's house tonight and we'll talk later."

"I can already tell I'm going to learn some new cusswords." Nap watched his father step onto the ladder. "Where're you going?"

"Well..." Jiggs climbed down the rungs. "I'd planned on getting water back on Starvation Creek today, but now I'm plastering a toilet. When I left Ox, he was lying down. I think he's bruised and won't admit it. If you go anywhere, see if he wants to go. His truck is out of commission."

"What's the matter with it?"

Jiggs paused on the ladder then climbed back up so he could see Nap. "There are things I need to talk to you about. Weird things that happened long ago—finding gold mines, moving frozen buildings, and missing dead people. We'll talk, but not tonight. I doubt if Ox will want to go to town today, but hide your truck keys—in case he tries to steal them."

"Holy monkeys!" Nap called after him. "Normal families don't do things like this. They work out their problems by throwing baseballs at each other."

"This is what happens. We're all getting older." Bazz sawed at the hole in the Bar and Grill's restroom with a utility knife, shaping it into a large rectangle.

"Speak for yourself." Jiggs looked at a piece of lumber, checking for cracks and knotholes. He'd pulled scraps from his woodpile. Every man in Two Pan had a stash of boards for make-do projects. They subscribed to the belief that there was no such thing as having too much lumber. The main threat to a cache was family. Kids stole cedar posts and plywood for treehouses and bridges. Wives used an expensive piece of oak or ash to prop up tomatoes or block raccoons from coming through the dog door. Without a wife or a fort-building boy, Jiggs' stockpile had grown to a proud size. He even had drywall and joint compound. "You want me to cut a couple of 2x4s to anchor that assist bar?"

"That'd be good." Bazz nodded.

Junior leaned against the door frame, watching the two men work. "Getting old is an angry process. You lose your friends and your memory. There's chronic pain. You become incontinent. Ordinary things change. There's a lot for you to get pissed about."

Jiggs paused sawing long enough to shoot Junior an irritated glance. "Stop using the word 'you' when you talk about aging."

"And the worst behavior is saved for those you're closest to." Junior stared at his father.

"Good thing we're not close, then." Bazz smiled at his son.

"Does Ox shower or bathe?" Junior asked.

"Good grief. How would I know?" Jiggs handed over the 2x4s he'd cut. "He smells like horse salve."

"As Ox ages, he loses more control," Junior said. Bazz began hammering the supports between studs. "Your dad is controlling what he can," Junior shouted. "Dressing. Refusing to bathe." Bazz grinned and banged the stud each time his son spoke.

"Why do you know this stuff?" Jiggs gave Bazz a piece of drywall.

"Before I came to this paradise, I worked for a senior care agency in L.A."

Bazz grinned. "Obviously, his patience and love of cranky people made him great at it. Here, stir up the joint compound." He shoved a bucket of powder at his son. "Add water and make it the consistency of mashed potatoes."

Each of them worked silently on their task until Jiggs asked, "So what am I supposed to do about Ox?" He handed Bazz pieces of joint tape.

"Don't nag. The more you badger him, the more he'll resist."

"And cuss," Jiggs said.

"That's enough damn stirring." Bazz reached for the bucket. "It's not a damn entry for a damn cake contest." He grinned at his son as he took the bucket.

"It's the anger and dementia that stimulates the swearing." Junior glared at his dad.

"Now don't nag and badger." Bazz used his tape knife to goop wet compound onto the patch. "What're you supposed to do instead of carp at us old people?"

"Distract them." Junior wiped his hands on a rag. "You could redirect Ox's mind. Bring up happy memories. If he's reminiscing, he's likely to forget what set him off. That's what I was trained to do, and it worked most of the time. If you have

questions, I could probably answer some of them over breakfast. I can make french toast kabobs with strawberries."

"I don't know what that is." Jiggs shook his head.

"French toast on a stick." Bazz rolled his eyes. "He's trying
to distract us."

"Does your dad see ghosts?" Junior asked.

Jiggs gathered tools, cleaning off white pieces of drywall as
he tossed them in the toolbox. "Good grief, I hope not."

"Does he hoard?"

Jiggs froze and looked at Junior.

"I'll make the french kabobs." He left for the kitchen.

"Don't pay him any mind." Bazz feathered the edges of the
patch into the wall. "He wants an excuse to cook gourmet stuff.
It's how he handles stress, but I'm supposed to be too old and
ignorant to know that."

"It's okay. He's given me a new plan to get information out
of Ox, but I'll stay and eat his fancy-pants pancakes. It's *my
way* of handling stress."

It's Not What You Say But How You Say It.

THE RAGGED PINNACLES of the Eagle Caps rose above the skyline, their crevices still white with snow. Considered upstarts on the geologic timeline, the peaks' granite shoulders cleaved the winds and thunderstorms that pestered them, making the land forget that at one time, this had been a tropical sea. At their feet, thick forests of fir and spruce drank the water they wept during the summer.

Spring came late to the Eagle Caps, but then, time can't be trusted here. It moves in fits and jumps...and sometimes...it doesn't move at all.

As Jiggs drove, a cool breeze rolled off the mountains, blowing through one window and out the other. Above, a hawk floated on the currents, its wings wide and unmoving.

He passed a pickup and trailer at the Silver Lake Trail head. The doors had been secured with a redneck lock. A chain and padlock ran through holes punched in the truck's body, binding the door. Beside the trailer, a bearded man loaded a llama with fishing gear.

Tourist season must be starting. It seemed early, but every year there were more people descending on the Wallowa range.

Thank the Lord time ran faster in the summer, as though the mountains pushed for winter to return.

Jiggs used the miles to think. Last week he was a native son of these hills, a descendent of pioneer stock who'd scratched out a living, had shaken a fist in the face of the Eagle Caps, and had endured to tell about it.

This week—he was a descendent of a German draft evader who'd stumbled into a ditch of gold and married a harlot. His ancestors had the backbone and smarts of dung beetles. Instead of grit and determination, his clan seemed to have ridden a party wagon willy-nilly into their future.

Except for Ox. His dad was the one kickback in the forefathers. The guy who had a map, knew his destination, and would punch anyone in his way. That left two possibilities for the skull: it was one of his dubious relatives or somebody else. If it were a stranger, there'd be no way he could discover who it was without involving forensics.

He suspected it was a relative. Somebody who'd done Ox harm. The only one he knew who'd made that kind of dent in his dad's life was Brick.

Last night, George had started to tell him about his granddad. Today, he'd get him to finish the story. If he were lucky, another piece of the mystery would fall into place. He hoped George wouldn't tell him he had aunts who were horse thieves or cousins who'd killed a congressman. Surely heaven set a limit on the black sheep assigned to one family.

As Jiggs turned into George's long driveway, a jackrabbit bounced across the road. He trailed it until braking to a stop in front of the ranch-style bungalow. He stared and mumbled, "Bound to happen." A black Dodge was parked in front of him—Nap's truck.

"Hey, Pop!" Nap sauntered onto the wide porch as Jiggs got out. "George says, 'Come on in.' What're you doing out here?"

116

"Probably the same thing as you." Jiggs walked up the ramp built over the steps.

Nap's eyes widened as he shook his head. "I doubt that."

"It's either drought or downpour!" George called from his big chair as Jiggs entered the living room. "Nobody's come to see me in months. Then I get three visitors in one day."

"Aren't you lucky?" They shook hands. "They're all Woolseys."

"By gum, this is a celebration." George pointed. "Nap, get us all a beer outta the fridge. There's chips and peanuts in the cabinet. Bring it all in. That Jason at Grubbs brings me groceries every week. He knows what's good to snack on."

"I bet he does," Nap mumbled, holding an imaginary joint to his lips as he went to the kitchen.

"I'll help you." Jiggs hurried out of the room as Ox began his rant about Grubbs. He looked around. "This place is tidier than ours."

"We must be pigs," Nap mumbled, looking in the fridge. He opened the door wide so his father could see the containers and sealed plastic bags stacked on the shelves. Each had a day of the week taped on it. "You want a beer, Gramps?" Nap yelled.

"I'd rather have a soda pop." His voice floated from the living room. Jiggs grabbed drinks. Nap announced, "Jackpot!" and pulled bags of chips, pretzels, and a gallon-sized can of mixed nuts from the cabinet over the dishwasher.

"Why're you out this way?" Ox eyed Jiggs as he handed him a can of root beer.

Jiggs hesitated. He'd thought of his excuse as he'd driven up, but he doubted if his dad would buy it. Instead he turned to George, "What do I owe you for dinner last night?"

"Nothin'. Not a thing." George closed his eyes, shook his head, and batted the question away. "I wish we'd get together for a meal more often. I enjoy good company."

"Me, too. It'll be my treat next time." Jiggs glanced at his dad. Everyone knew George wouldn't take money, but an offer had been made. A tentative reckoning of the books. The reason *why* George was left holding the bill sat down in the room with them. An awkward silence bounced between the men. Nap walked in and spread the snacks and pickings on the coffee table.

"Hey. This looks good." George clapped his thick hands together. "Where're you goin? Aren't you joining us?"

Nap had stuffed a handful of peanuts in his mouth and was headed for the door. "After I finish."

"I hired him to cut the limbs and brush around here. Fire threat. I can't keep up with it anymore." George wrenched the cap off his beer.

"You're not paying him," Jiggs said. "He'll gladly do that for a neighbor."

Nap stuck his head back through the doorway. "George, I think you should convince Dad of our plan."

Ox waved him away. "Get the hell outta here and go work." Nap disappeared.

"What plans?"

Ox shook peanuts in his palm so they rolled into his fingers. He popped them into his mouth one at a time. "It's nothin'. He's just bein' stupid."

"Seems that stupid runs in the family. What's going on?"

Ox shrugged. "I only came with Nap to visit my neighbor."

An impish smile twitched at George's mouth. "We're gonna blow up that tree blocking Starvation Creek."

Jiggs rubbed his forehead. "Not you, too."

"I've got the dynamite." George nodded so hard the jowls of his cheeks jiggled. "We used to blow stumps and log jams when I worked timber. It'll move that baby out of the way. Piece of cake."

"Craphouse crickets! Tell me you don't have twenty-year-old dynamite around here in some shed. Do you?"

"Oh, settle down. It's perfectly safe. I've handled the stuff all my life. It's not dangerous unless you do something stupid."

"Don't tell him anything." Ox scowled. "He'd call the sheriff or notify the government if a cow looked at him cross-eyed."

"Excuse me for saying this, George..." Jiggs scooted in his chair so he was squared off, facing the big man and not his father. "But I've been up to that downed tree. It's steep. There's no trail and no solid footing. How are you going to get up there to place a charge?"

"I can teach Nap."

"Mother Mary and Joseph!" Jiggs leaned back, blinking.

"He wants to do it," George said. "I was that age when I learned. He's nimble and smart. He'll be fine. Every man should know how to handle dynamite. Comes in handy."

"I agree, but teetering on the side of a hill shouldn't be his first place to experiment. Where are you going to be while Nap is trying to run across a moving rockslide? You're won't be up there with him, and you can't be below in case this ridge slides down on top of you. I'm telling you this is a bad idea," Jiggs said to George's downturned face.

"Maybe you have a point," Ox said. "Which is hard to believe since you're about as sharp as a marble."

Jiggs ignored his dad. "We'll do this job the old-fashioned way. First, we'll cut the tree up." He pounded his palm with the side of his hand, emphasizing each step. "Then we'll use your mules to move the root ball. Lastly we'll dig the channel out by hand and dam up the sides, forcing water to flow back downstream. Nobody's blowing anything up. That whole ridge could come sliding down right over this property."

"Well, it's gotta be done soon. The side streams are dryin' up. The cattle are runnin' out of water." George shrugged. "But

I guess it don't matter. My kids don't want the ranch, only the money. Let it dry up and go to weeds."

"No—because I want to buy it." Jiggs' voice was louder than he'd meant it to be. It took a moment for the volume to fade.

Ox stared at him. "What do you want with this place?"

"Crap, Dad. Really?" Jiggs stood. "Excuse me, George. I'm gonna step outside, before I open my mouth and regret it later."

"Too late for that," Ox called after him.

Jiggs stood on the porch, looking at the limbs and brush Nap had cleared from the front of the house. He wasn't sure what fumed him more: using his son to set explosives, or having his dad question his drive and goals. Why was it hard for Ox to believe that his son wanted to add land? To be the biggest rancher in the county someday? And why was Ox here on the day he'd come to milk information out of George about Brick? His dad was a constant burr under his blanket.

He walked around the side of the house where Nap was raking the weeds he'd cut away from the foundation. "You want some cheap help?"

Nap looked up. "Oh man. I can tell by your face, they told you about the dynamite."

Jiggs shook his head. "And your grandfather calls *me* a moron." He pointed. "Poison oak over here."

"I saw it," Nap said.

Jiggs went to an open shed and made a sprayer of weed killer. He dosed the poison oak and walked along the fence line, spraying plants. When he returned, Nap was working at the back of the house, running the weedwacker around a huge lilac bush. "I've settled down now. I think I'm ready to go back inside." He set the sprayer on the deck. "Have you ever tried to make a business deal with heckling from the sidelines?"

"You're tough, Dad." His son gave him a thumbs up. "As my ag-econ professor used to tell us before a big test,...'Turn your papers over, and whoop ass.'"

Jiggs walked back into the living room. Both men stopped talking and looked up. He sat down. A stumbling silence wandered between them. "Nap is about half-way finished," he finally said.

"Now—I'm gonna pay him..." George began.

"No. You won't." Impatience pricked Jiggs' words. "Many was the time Pax or I needed to check the west side of Starvation Creek. We'd catch one of your horses and bareback him wherever we needed to go. Return him the next day. You never told dad or complained. Your wife always brought us lemonade and cake whenever we were here, fixing fence. I remember all of us haying at night and having picnics on the tailgate in the dark. Some of my family's best times were on your ranch." Jiggs saw Ox's face soften and the lines disappear between his eyebrows. A wrinkled corner of his mouth turned up along with a memory playing across his eyes.

"Dad, maybe I should've discussed bank accounts before I said anything to George. But I thought it'd be right to buy this land." Several heartbeats passed. Finally Jiggs said, "Hey!"

Ox twitched as though he'd been poked with a hoof pick. "What? What'd you say?"

"I said," Jiggs' voice amped up louder, "George told me last night that his kids weren't coming back. I thought we should sound him out about buying it."

"Before you came in, Ox and I were talking..." George said, "about the same thing. I hadn't thought of selling, until lately. A realtor called, representing some fellas I let elk hunt here a few seasons ago. I told him absolutely not. So when you mentioned it, I was throwed-off, but now that you've opened the gate, let's see how it is. What're you suggesting?"

Jiggs looked at the floor and rubbed his hand over his mouth. "Well exactly how many grazing acres do you have here?"

"Heaven help us." Ox's head rocked back as he looked at the ceiling. "Never ask a question you don't already know the answer. That's like asking, 'How old is that horse?' Don't trust a fella to tell you. You gotta check the nag's teeth before you start."

"George isn't going to lie."

"You want to learn how to trade or not? Never come at it head on."

"Okay, George." Jiggs looked at the big man. "Have you re-seeded the grass in those east pastures?"

"Hell. You know he has." Ox threw up his hands. "You can tell by hanging your head out the pickup and lookin'. But you don't pay attention to anythin' except the dirt in front of you when you're drivin'."

Jiggs took a breath and let it out slowly. "Are you gonna do this the whole time? You can't stay out of it, can you?"

"Ask the questions right. It's all in how you say it. Better yet, don't ask anything at all. You're just pissin' people off, actin' like a rube."

Jiggs lifted his hat and scrubbed his hand through his hair. "Tell you what. Why don't you give it a go, Dad. I'll try to learn something."

"Sheee-it. You never learned a thing from me in your life. But if you want to start now, pay attention."

Jiggs sat back in the arm chair, a beer in one hand and a bag of Doritos on his lap. Earlier when he'd talked with Junior, he wondered what happy times he could bring up to distract his dad. To his knowledge, Ox had never lived a happy day in his life.

The two old men were busy joking and jabbering back and forth. Jiggs noticed not one cussword came out of Ox. Not one hint that George would be leaving his land to the main Woolsey idiot. Junior was right. Let Ox reminisce about good times. And Ox's good times seemed to be centered on building an empire to shame his father.

Jiggs wondered if he could work this magic meeting to get what he wanted, too.

"Okay. I think it's a good deal on both sides. It's time to go." Ox stood up.

George extended his hand. "So I'm stayin' here 'til I'm ready to move in with my kids. When that happens, you're the guys I'll sell to. Is this good enough for a contract?"

"Your word has always been gold." Ox shook on it. "Let's go, Jiggs. Never hang around after closin' the deal. It gives the other party time to change their minds."

"Nap's not done," Jiggs said. "I can hear him on the roof, sweeping branches off. He can take you home. I've got other business to tend to."

"Like what?" Ox stared.

Jiggs stared back. Thoughts circled his mind that he'd like for George to finish his story of how Brick had died. He studied his dad for a moment. He wouldn't get any information if his dad were here. "Never mind." He grabbed chip sacks and pushed empty beer bottles into Ox's hands. "We'll clear the mess we've made."

"Don't worry about it. I got a gal who comes in twice a week. She'll get it."

Jiggs herded Ox in front of him toward the kitchen. "She does a good job. Can I get her name?"

"Why?" Ox squinted. "You've got a son to do housework. That's what I made you and Pax do."

"Yeah, that's another great memory."

In ten minutes they were driving away. Nap had given his best hang-dog impression, apologizing that there was too much to do there, and he'd be late for the Great-Clean-Out at Ox's house. But not to worry. He'd eat in town, or with George, or anywhere in the county besides home.

A Clean House is The Sign of A Boring Person

AS THEY PULLED into the gravel drive, Jiggs broke the silence of the trip home. "I would've bought the land now. George might change his mind. Why wait?"

"You're a jackrabbit, hopping to the next big idea so you can mess it up. George won't change his mind. He's not like you." Ox gave him a warning stare. "You don't push a man off his land. Everybody wants old people to get out of the way. George built that ranch. He'll stay as long as he wants. When he's ready, he'll sell to us, and we'll keep it goin'."

Jiggs glanced at him. Ox was right about doing homework before jumping into a land deal. He doubted his dad knew if there was enough money in the savings account. At least they hadn't saddled themselves with debt. No telling what he would discover when he pried the finances away from his dad. He motioned toward the small house. "You want to eat before we start cleaning out your badger nest or take a break in the middle?"

"Leave everything the way it is." Ox scowled.

"Wouldn't you enjoy some home-cooked meals in your fridge? That's what George had. You could heat up a plate of pot roast or meatloaf whenever you wanted."

Ox fiddled with a buttonhole on his shirt, looking for a missing button.

"Well, whether you like it or not, I'm having someone come in to fix a few meals and do a little cleaning."

"They can cook. That's all."

"The hash-slinging tent at round-up is cleaner than your kitchen. Nobody's going to set foot in there if we don't unpollute it. Mom's yelling in heaven right now about the stink in your sink."

Ox gave a slow headshake. "She could voice her opinion. That's for sure." He pulled the door latch. "Just the kitchen. That's all."

Jiggs scrambled out of the pickup, remembering Ox's advice, "Get goin' before they change their mind."

"Why in God's green earth do you need twenty or thirty of these?" Jiggs shook a nested stack of shallow aluminum pans which had once held grocery-store sweet rolls. He winged them across the kitchen into the thirty-two-gallon trash can that he'd rolled into the dining area.

"They're handy." Ox pulled the containers out of the bin, bending them back into shape and slapping them on the counter. "I'll be usin' these to hold parts for my bench if you'd ever get out of here and let me work on it."

"Go out there now. That'd lower my blood pressure considerably."

"All this stuff you wanna throw away is worth somethin'. People will pay money for it if we ever have a junk sale."

"Son of a monkey!" Jiggs pulled an owl decoy out of a cabinet and shook it. "I've been looking for this. Why's it in your kitchen?" Ox moved magazines around on the table. "Hey!" Jiggs called louder and more annoyed. "What's this doing here?" His words and tone were the same as he'd used when Nap was ten years old. Jiggs would find broken dishes or a melted hair brush or other evidence of boyhood experiments stashed behind curtains and under couches, then forgotten.

"The owl scares mice," Ox mumbled. "It's under control. I run my mouse trap-lines every morning. Why do you think I use so much peanut butter?"

"Gimme a break!" Jiggs threw the owl at the trash can. He'd have to get it out later—when Ox wasn't looking—but for the moment, he felt like throwing something.

"Sounds like a football game goin' on in here." Nap came through the door, leaving it open behind him. "I could hear the shouting and grunting from my truck."

"Glad to see you. Pick a team." Jiggs turned back to the cabinet.

"Dammit. We need more gravel. I didn't hear you drive up." Ox stood at the table, sifting through newspapers.

Jiggs threw a dark look at his son. "I thought you weren't coming."

"Finished early. Didn't wanna miss all this fun." He pulled the owl from the can, and held it up, giving Ox a questioning look.

"Your father ditched it, not me." Ox looked to heaven as though reminding the Lord that His plans—whatever they were—weren't working. "If your dad had an ounce of sense, he'd put that owl in the maple tree to scare off his crows in the mornings."

"I'm keeping this." Nap tucked the decoy under his arm and began digging through the trash.

Jiggs crossed the room. "I'll trade you places. Get over there and clean out cabinets." He quietly added, "Keep your grand-dad occupied. I'm going to look at the ledger." He tried to pull the owl from Nap's armlock, but the boy twisted and blocked him.

"No worries." Nap grinned.

"Watch out for mouse traps. Clean up their crap. There's Lysol next to the sink." Jiggs grinned back at him and turned on his boot heel.

"Where're you goin'?" Ox watched him walk toward the hallway.

"When's the last time you changed your sheets? Or did a load of laundry?"

"Yesterday!"

Jiggs barked a laugh. He stepped into the alcove with the roll top desk, listening to the voices drift from the kitchen-dining area.

"This is cool, Gramps. What is it?"

"It used to hang over the kitchen table."

Jiggs pushed the licorice drops and almonds off the ledger and flipped to the Expenses section.

"Are these the Budweiser Clydesdales?"

"Yep. They used to circle the outside of the lamp when you turned it on. Doesn't work anymore."

Ox's scratchy handwriting listed each bill, until the last few months. Jiggs flipped pages back and forth. Entries became messy. Numbers were scratched out or written over.

"These horses are really detailed, aren't they? Maybe I can fix it. Where'd you get it?"

"A hotel. Your grandma and I were in Lewiston, buying cattle. We drove past a little flophouse goin' outta business. She just had to stop. Said she always wanted some hotel art." A door squeaked open then shut.

"That's it? That's the art she wanted? A fish drinking a beer?"

Jiggs' stomach growled. He tossed almonds in his mouth as he lifted and inspected papers. Scattered between auction ads and equipment catalogs were envelopes from the county assessor, Tracy's feed store, and Minam State Bank. He began searching drawers.

"It's a collector's item. Where else could you get a fish in a suit, slurping Ol' Milwaukee? It made her laugh."

"I wish I could've known her. Where's a screwdriver? I see a wire loose on this lamp. Maybe I can get it working again. We could hang it and the fish picture."

The rustle of the junk drawer covered part of Ox's words. "...and if I don't hold onto the bygone...the memories will be lost. I want you to know about this..." Another cabinet door opened and closed.

Jiggs let out a silent groan, discovering the file of bank deposits. A three-month-old check for steers they'd sold was paper-clipped to the outside—never deposited. He sat on the edge of the desk, scrubbing his hand through his hair. He couldn't even get stacks of newspapers from his dad, how was he going to take away the books?

"Everybody leaves something when they die," Ox was saying. "This is a bowl my mom had. Used to be, the Jewel Tea man went door to door selling tea leaves, coffee beans, and dinnerware. Out here, women were miles from neighbors. So the Jewel Tea man's visit was something to look forward to. I can't imagine how long it took her to save for this bowl. I'm guessing it was the only nice dish she ever had. It's the only thing left that shows she ever existed."

"You're the evidence, Gramps. You had to come from somewhere."

Silence, then Ox's heavy sigh filtered down the hallway. "You need to have something your ancestors touched and used. That's where legacy lives. That's why I want to leave you with a ranch. You can't do anything if you don't have land." His voice took on the drained tiredness of a man who'd rolled the boulder up the hill too many times. "But we pay for what our ancestors did."

"What'd ya mean, Gramps?"

"I mean, you gotta save every penny you can. You never know what's gonna come flyin' at you and change your future. What's taking your dad so long?"

"Hey, what're these?" Nap's voice had a light, change-of-subject tone.

Jiggs hurried to the bedroom, grabbing the shirts, jeans, and underwear draped across furniture. He flung them in the middle of the sheets. With several yanks, he stripped the bedding off the mattress and wadded it into a big ball. Trying not to make a sound, he walked on the balls of his feet, toting the sheets down the hallway. Quickly, he stepped through the arched doorway of the alcove. He stuffed envelopes and the check into the sheets. His hand was on the ledger...

"What the hell are you doin'? The bed isn't in here," Ox growled.

Jiggs turned, tossing almonds into his mouth. "I'm hungry."

"You can have those." Ox watched him for a moment. Then he moved back and waved him out of the room. "I already sucked the chocolate offa them."

Jiggs' eyes widened as he tongued nutmeats into his cheek like a squirrel. As soon as he stepped out the door, he spit in the weeds.

Nap's voice followed him across the gravel drive. "Where's Dad goin?"

"To do a load of laundry and gargle, I suspect." Ox laughed like old men do when they watch someone else fall down.

"Do you want these little ceramic figures?" Nap called out.

"Naw. I don't know where they came from. Look like turds. Bury 'em out back. That'll make some scientist scratch his head and get a government grant when he digs 'em up two hundred years from now." Ox snorted another chuckle.

"I made these for you..." Nap said. "In Fourth grade."

"You want 'em back? You can have 'em."

"As the Old Crow Caws The Young Crow Learns"

—Irish Saying

THE NEXT MORNING a cacophony of cawing awakened Jiggs. It sounded like a gaggle of witches screeching and hollering through the scratchy speakers of the Two Pan Rodeo Arena. He ignored it as he scrambled a half-dozen eggs and stuck bread in the toaster.

Nap wandered into the kitchen in pajama bottoms, yawning, "What's with your alarm? I hadn't planned on getting up at the break of day."

"Must be mating season." Jiggs slid the carafe under the coffeemaker. "Something's got them excited."

"Oh shit!" Nap ran out the backdoor, bare-chested and bare-footed. Jiggs stared for a moment then followed.

Ox stood on the gravel drive, his hands on his hips. As soon as Jiggs appeared, he retreated to his front stoop. With a single wave, he grinned, and went inside.

Jiggs turned to stare at the black mass flittering among the maple leaves. At least fifty birds squawked from the limbs. Without warning, three or four feathered bodies dived into the branches.

"They're having a shit-fit." Nap watched, open-mouthed. "I didn't know it would do that." Another squadron of crows dive bombed the branches.

"What'd you do?"

"I climbed up there last night and tied the owl to a limb. Gramps said it'd keep them out of the tree."

"You have a bachelor's of science in Agriculture and Bullshit and still don't know to ignore anything that old man says?" Jiggs nudged Nap, directing his attention to the small house. Ox was watching from the window and laughing. "Get the owl down."

A larger murder of crows mobbed the tree again, pecking and scratching as they flew by. Two flew over the owl, dropping sticks.

"I'll get the shotgun. It'll run them off for a while, but I'm not climbing up there until nightfall."

"Ignore it. C'mon, let's go eat. We're not putting on a show for your granddad's entertainment." He walked inside. "I doubt if there'll be anything left of that decoy by the end of the day."

They heard Ox before they saw him. He whistled a nameless tune as he came through the mudroom, into the kitchen, and sat in his usual chair, his legs extended into the room. Jiggs and Nap kept eating. "Well, this is a somber group," he said. "I'm glad everybody's up early. We got things to do today." He winked at his grandson.

Nap gave him a stony stare. "You told me the decoy would keep the crows outta the tree."

"No, I didn't." Ox held up his hand as though swearing on a Bible or making a "halt" signal—or both. "What I *said* was...'the owl would *scare* the crows.' And they're scared all right." His voice picked up speed. His dive-bombing gestures became animated. "Did you see 'em? A big owl like that will kill and eat a crow for breakfast. They're born enemies. Like Superman and...well...whoever the hell Superman fights." He laughed and gave a single clap as he straightened in his chair. "More and more of 'em will keep coming from miles around, taking turns mobbing that decoy. Speaking of breakfast, whattya got? You cleaned out my ice box last night. I got nothin' to eat."

Jiggs waved a fork toward the skillet of eggs they'd left for him. Ox filled his plate and coffee mug and sat back down. "So who's taking me to town today?" Nap and Jiggs exchanged glances and continued eating.

"Since you're in such a good mood, Gramps, I've got a subject to discuss." Jiggs looked up, trying to stare Nap into silence.

"Let 'er rip." Ox shoveled eggs into his mouth.

"You read the ag magazines. You know how genetic improvements can make a herd more profitable, don't you?" Ox didn't say anything. "It'll improve the yield of our beef over fifty percent. We can produce much more and not have to run as many cows. There's less expense in vet bills, feed costs, transport—"

"Says you," Ox interrupted. "What do you know? College education didn't even teach you about crows."

"If we were breeding crows for market," Nap said, staring at his granddad, "then I'd learn everything there was to know about them. As it is, I'm a rancher. I know beef."

"Bull shit. Billy has all the genetics we need. He turns out calves that are tough enough to survive on this land. It's taken years to cultivate his traits. You don't see half of my calf-crop dying through the winter. Your man-made calves will have pneumonia with the first snowfall. They wouldn't even live long enough to make a decent hot dog."

"BillyBull has had his run. We need to be making changes in carcass-fat composition now. A genetically superior bull will sire at least ninety calves over the next three to five years, and easily pay for itself, producing more pounds for years."

Ox pointed a fork at Nap. "When I first came here, all I had was twenty dollars and a crazy mule that didn't know its name."

"I thought you were born here," Nap said.

"I left and came back. What I'm saying is—"

"Where'd you go?" Jiggs said.

"None of your damned business." Ox thumped the table with the side of his hand. "The point I'm making is there was nothing left of the original homestead except a share-picker's acre and a three-teated milk cow. I slept in the dirt. Got snake-bit. A scorpion stung me on the lip. It turned purple, abscessed and had to be drained. This ear got ripped up in the backlash of a barbwire fence. Nothing stopped me. I tied a bandana around whatever was bleedin', maimed or fallin' off, and I kept buying land and cattle. I made the Rockin' W what it is. You don't know diddle about ranching. And *I'm sayin'*—we're not getting any robot-designed bulls."

"If you understood what I was talking about, you wouldn't be so quick to condemn it. I want what's best for—"

"You want what's easiest!" Ox pounded the table. "When it's your land and your legacy, then you can make the decisions, and I wish you luck. I really do. But honestly, you don't need to worry about it. Your father jumps without looking. He'll lose everything before your hair-brained idea to get a damn designer bull can ever happen."

Silence smothered the air out of the room. Even the cawing of the crows seemed muted.

Nap slowly let out his breath and looked at his dad. "You gonna let him talk to you like that?"

Jiggs closed his eyes, his mouth flat lined as he tossed his fork onto his plate. "Well, this is a family moment we'll remember for a while. It's like being a little kid again and starting the morning with an Ox Woolsey pep talk. Boy, those were the days. The problem is, Nap, I've heard this 'screw-up' speech for about thirty years. I've learned to ignore it. It's the same as that god-awful racket the crows are making. A bunch of hoodoo over nothing. But..."

He turned to face his dad, his eyes narrowing. "Ox, you should realize that things have changed. I'm not a little kid anymore. It's low, even for you, to come into a man's house and insult him in front of his son. That's a line I never thought you'd cross. And you..." Jiggs looked at his son. "What do you want me to do? Punch him in the face? Grab him by the short hairs and throw him out the door? That's a line *I'm* not going to cross. He's old and he's sick and he's still my father."

"Ugggh. Shit." Ox stood. "What a bunch of gum-bleedin' righteousness. Your ass was hauled into the principal's office every other day for makin' somebody's nose bloody. Go ahead and *try* to teach me a lesson. Besides...this isn't your house." He circled his arm, looking around him. "I built all this—" He hesitated, took two steps, and pulled a metal cracker tin out of the trash. "What the hell is this doin' here?"

"It's always bugged me. I threw it away last night," Jiggs said.

"You take any more of my stuff, and I'll rip off both your ears to match mine." Ox turned and stomped out the door, carrying the tin labeled: STRINGS TOO SHORT TO USE.

Jiggs left the dishes on the table. He needed to be doing something—anything. He moved his Ford so the front wheels were on the terrace behind the house, leaving a large gap under the truck. The engine ran while he carried tools from the garage.

"Whaddya doin?" Nap walked out the patio door and down the incline.

"I'm kind of in a hurry. About fifteen things need to get done today."

"So you're changing oil? Now?"

135

"Yep." Jiggs switched off the ignition, lay on a feed sack, and pushed himself under the truck. "It's an hour and a half 'til the bank opens. I need to keep busy or my thoughts go to dark places."

"What'd you mean the other day when you said we needed to talk about gold and dead bodies?"

"Old history. When I find the answers, I'll tell you. Right now, we have bigger snakes to kill. Hand me the wrench and lean down here. You're going to be busy."

In a moment, Nap was on the ground, sliding under the truck from the passenger side, pushing the oil pan into place. "How in the world did you survive growing up?"

"Don't worry about that now. It wasn't all yelling and ducking." Jiggs cranked the drain plug, letting it *clank* into the pan. A black-brown stream followed it.

"Do you have even *one* good childhood memory?"

"Yep." The silence reeled out, as Jiggs worked on unscrewing the filter.

Finally Nap asked, "Well, what was it?"

"Riding. Campfires. Unimportant moments. Dad was too busy to pay attention to us when we were little. He didn't act like that around Mom. She didn't put up with it. When her heart gave out, Pax was sixteen. I was thirteen. Dad said she was carrying too much to deal with. That made us boys feel like crap, but we figured it was him who'd worried her into the grave. It wasn't until after she was gone that we caught the full lick of his belt. Now that I'm older, I suppose I can understand. He didn't know what to do with us besides teach us how to survive. And, of course, there was only one way to do that..."

"His way," Nap said, watching the last of the oil drip from the opening.

"I couldn't wait to get out of here as fast as I could and get my own place. Then life got in the way. Guilt is powerful glue."

"How so?"

"My brother died. I couldn't abandon Ox and this ranch. I did what I had to do. Then I got married at twenty-one, and life kept on happening." He looked at Nap. "Your mother often reminded me, that I didn't have to turn out like Ox. I could be a better father. I've tried. 'Course, that's not setting the bar very high."

"You're a good dad. None of my friends had the chance to go to college or create new herds. I don't know that I could've sacrificed what you have." Nap noodled his fingers in the oil pan, found the plug, and screwed it back in.

"Well, part of your opportunities are due to the ranch Ox built up."

"Last night, after you left, Gramps told me stories. I worked on his lamp." Nap rubbed oil on the gasket of the new filter. "It amazed me. He seemed normal and decent. As a little kid, I was always afraid of him. And now this morning...with anybody else that owl decoy joke would've been funny, but with him, it seemed mean. I don't see how he can be decent one minute, then explode into a bastard. Why's he so pissed at you all the time?"

"Because I'm the one that's left." Jiggs took the new filter and screwed it into place. "He favored Pax, no doubt about it. But Pax crashed his truck four years after Mom died. He inconsiderately passed away before Dad had planned. That left only me around. Who else can he rant to?" Jiggs shook his head. "There's been some moments. Boy oh boy."

Nap lay still, looking at the undercarriage of the pickup. "When I was little, I was jumping around the house, making stupid fart noises. Gramps was in the living room with me. I could tell I was bothering him, because he took his pipe out of his mouth and gave me one of those stares like he was melting me with fire. You know what I mean?"

Jiggs scooched out from under the truck, and Nap wriggled out from beneath the passenger side. "Yep. I know those looks," he said as he unscrewed the cap from a canister of 10W40 and poured it into the engine.

"I stuck my tongue out at him. Can you believe it? I was a bold little shit back then." Nap uncapped and readied another quart. "Then I turned my back so I didn't have to see his laser glare, and I kept bouncing. Mom yelled from the kitchen, telling me to stop. So I made louder noises. I was hopping, bumping off furniture and all of a sudden my arm felt scalded. I was on the floor, rolling and screaming. Mom came running in. There was a round, red burn on my arm. Gramps seemed shocked and surprised. He guessed I'd bounced right into his pipe. I argued that he did it on purpose. I was snottin' and cryin'. It hurt like I'd been stuck with a branding iron. Mom wouldn't listen. Said it was my fault. I've thought about it since then. I figured I must've remembered it wrong. You know how a little kid blames everybody else. But I've still kept my distance from him."

"It sounds exactly like something the jackass would do." Jiggs wiped the dipstick, stuck it in its tube, and pulled it again. "I'm sorry I didn't know about that."

"Sometime later, I buried that pipe." Nap stared at his dad. "He looked for it for days."

"I remember that." Jiggs dropped the hood then pressed it until it clicked. "I'm sorry to tell you this, but you probably saved his life. He quit smoking after that."

Jiggs took a shower, dressed, and checked his watch. Time was stuck again. He glanced at the sky. The light slanting through the maple made promises, but it gave no hints if they were good or bad. He poured a cup of coffee and paced the patio to wait it out. Time had to move on eventually.

Nap came from the garage, wiping his hands on a rag. "Are you anxious because of the books? Is that why you're goin' to the bank as soon as the doors open?"

"We've got to fix Starvation Creek, today, or we'll have cattle in a lot of trouble. George will too. The side springs are drying up." He checked the sky then his watch again. "But that ledger was a mess. I think he has dementia or early Alzheimer's. I have no idea if we have money or if the bills have been paid. I tried to be calm about it this morning so he wouldn't get suspicious and start hiding papers. I'm going to the bank and see if I can make heads or tails of it from there. Whatever you do, don't throw anything out."

"We only wrangled one sack of newspapers out of him."

"That's good. We'll tackle that later." Jiggs looked at the sky again. "To heck with it. I'm leaving now. I'll bang on their door. I'm sure Little McGinty gets there early to count his money. You," Jiggs pointed, "load up the chain saw, ropes, and shovel. Start cutting the tree in the creek. I'll be there to help as soon as I can. We'll borrow George's mules and drag the stump out then dig the channel so all the water flows back down the stream."

"George and I talked about another plan last night."

"What?" Jiggs stared at his son.

"Now don't get 'Ox Woolsey' on me. Just listen, okay?"

"Always Obey Your Parents—When They Are Present"

—Mark Twain

NAP GLANCED AT his father then studied the cracks in the concrete patio. "After I finished at George's last night, he tried to pay me." His hand quickly shot up, cutting off his dad's words. "I didn't take his money. Instead...well, we vetoed your objections about the quick way to fix that creek. He gave me a quarter stick of dynamite."

A line of fury creased his dad's forehead. His eyes could've driven nails.

"I already know you think it's too dangerous," Nap quickly added. "And it's illegal to do it on government land, but...Gramps thinks it's a good idea, too." He glanced toward the crows mobbing the decoy. "Well, you probably think the crow-thing should tell me something about Gramps' ideas." He widened his stance, feeling his father's stare bulldoze against him. "But people have been clearing stumps this way for years. We're gonna set off a charge on flat ground. A practice blast, so I can learn, before doing it up on the hillside. George will supervise. I know he can't climb the ridge, but he'll be below, watching the whole..." The words stuck in his throat. The last time he'd said them was to Audie Dodge.

Actually, he'd screamed them from the bottom of his lungs. He still carried the image of the broken leather strap lying in the dirt.

Audie had bragged about making catapults in Scouts. They'd snuck off to the south pasture and built a souped-up contraption using a car spring to get extra yardage. It happened so quickly neither boy knew what was occurring. Nap was still loading the pouch when the restraining strap broke. The concrete-block counterweight whizzed past within an inch of his ear.

"Son of a bitch!" He'd screamed. Audie blinked from the force of Nap's breath so close to his face. "You were supposed to be watching!" Even as he was yelling, Nap could hear the fear in his voice. He could imagine his head, mashed like one of those animals smeared on the road. "I thought you knew what you're doing!" He'd tried to make his words angry, but his voice cracked like a thirteen-year-old's first-shocked meeting with reality.

Nap let out a long slow breath. He wanted to focus somewhere besides his feet, but his dad's stare showered over him, dampening his palms and armpits.

"Okay. Okay. Maybe dynamite isn't the most brilliant idea. I suppose it *is* dangerous. I'll get the chainsaw and cut slabs off the damn tree. It's gonna take forever, though." He turned and walked away, wondering if his father's hands were still clenching and unclenching. He didn't look back. "But it woulda been cool," he muttered to himself.

Little Bill McGinty pushed a printout of the Rockin' W's checking account across the desk. "What makes you think your dad is losing it?" he grunted.

Jiggs tapped the date at the top of the paper and pushed it back with an impatient frown. He'd driven the twenty-one miles to Minam National Bank in twenty minutes. After beating on the door, Little McGinty let him wait in the lobby. The stuffed and mounted heads of antelope, deer, and elk watched him until the banker could 'clear his desk.' None of the McGintys were hunters. They had only contributed one head to the collection, but they encouraged their customers to bring in their mounted kills for a brief display period. They discovered the rotating show of dead animals encouraged business. Folks liked to wander into the bank to see a 10-point buck or the "one that didn't get away."

"Oh. I misunderstood," Little McGinty mumbled. "You wanted this month's statement." He punched a few keys on his computer. Beside him, a printer whirred into action. "Yeah, my Dad's still coming in every day. Even at ninety he can catch an error in a teller's receipt. It's pretty amazing."

Jiggs wore a *bully-for-him-how-does-that-help-me* stare.

"You remember the time your dad brought a heifer into the bank?" McGinty tapped his pen on the desk, with a faraway look as though pulling the memory from his brain vault. "Said he was making a loan payment."

Jiggs reached and grabbed the first sheets from the printer. He didn't want to hear the story. And it would go on forever if he allowed Little McGinty to pick up the papers one at a time, tap them on the desk, straightening the edges, and then place the staple, just so, in the corner. Heaven help him, but bankers were nitpickers. He flipped through the documents, looking for the ending balance.

"That calf made a mess right there in the lobby." Little McGinty pointed. "Ox was breaking in a new ag-lending officer, Skel Burke. He was green and starting out. The economy had tanked. Nobody was buying cattle, and Ox had a loan payment due. I can still see your face. You walked in, looked at the situation, and froze like you'd been hit with a bucket of ice water. I was a teller...what were we then? About ninteen?"

"I don't remember." Jiggs nabbed the next batch of papers getting pushed out of the printer.

"Ox was cussing you. The calf was at the end of the tether, doing a little dance, spooked. Skel was trying to herd all of you into a corner, away from customers. Ox kept saying animals were his currency and the ranch his bank. His money was spread over a thousand acres, and if Skel kept demanding immediate payment or foreclosure, he could 'damn well take a cow or allow an extension.' Ox was growling back and forth, dragging that calf between teller windows."

Jiggs flipped from page to page, trying to ignore the jabber. In high school, Little McGinty had been one of those kids who'd been quick to point out the rules. He used to snitch on others. Jiggs had tried to help him outgrow the tendency by thumping it out of him.

"Ox was raising such a fuss, it made Dad come out of his office. I remember he whispered to me, 'Watch carefully. This is how to call a customer's bluff.' Without a word, he took that calf and led it back to the vault. And he was right. Ox asked for a receipt and didn't say another word. It was over in a second."

"I guess all's well that ends well, then." Jiggs gave Little McGinty a meaningless smile. "I need copies of the savings account, too."

The banker punched more keys on his computer. "So what's Ox done that makes you think he's losing it now?"

Jiggs stared at his old classmate. He'd grown into a round-bellied, bald, son of a banker. A farmer's tan and a few more wallops would've helped him be a different fellow. "Dad lost his statements. It's worrying him. As you pointed out, he's very watchful of his money."

"Sorry." Little McGinty stared at the screen. "There are three savings accounts. You're not on any of them. I can't give you a statement."

"You're kidding?" Jiggs stared. "I'm a stockholder here. It's not like I'm a stranger trying to hoodwink anybody and steal something."

Little McGinty shrugged. "It's the law. I could mail them to Ox if that would help."

"Oh, that'd be dandy." Jiggs gathered the papers in front of him. "I get the mail out of the box every day. It'll cost you money to send it, and I'll open it up and look at it tomorrow."

"Or Ox could call. I can tell him over the phone if you don't do online banking." Jiggs let out a laugh. A frown shadowed Little McGinty's face. "You don't remember the calf incident?"

Jiggs cocked his head, seesawing between the truth that Ox had pulled one over on Big McGinty and the thought that he might need another loan someday. The episode was one of the few laughs he and his father shared.

Ox had taken a runt calf into the bank, not because he thought they'd keep it, but because it was the smallest and easiest to handle. He'd gotten the idea when he read about a rancher in western Oregon who'd been foreclosed. He'd driven his entire herd into the bank's lobby to deliver them.

When Big McGinty met Ox's bluff, the banker had taken a cull heifer, a slow-growing peewee. The banker had planned on it temporarily residing in the field behind his house. Future steaks for his freezer. But his family had other intentions. They named the cow Larry, and she lived a long and healthy life. Ox and Jiggs had a quiet laugh each time they went to the bank. There on the wall, was McGinty's only contribution to the stuffed head collection—an old Angus with a gold nameplate: Larry.

Jiggs gave a regretful wag of his head. He held out his hand as though offering condolences. "Thanks for opening early. Sorry. I don't remember the particular story you're telling. Maybe Dad and I are both losing it."

*

Jiggs stopped by the Latte Da coffee shop and picked up a couple of ham sandwiches before he drove home. With Little McGinty's yapping, it'd been difficult to look at the checking account. All he wanted to find out was how close they were to the bottom of the barrel. He still didn't know. There were funds in checking, but he had no idea if they were underwater on the bills.

All the way home he rehearsed what he was going to tell Ox. It was time to let go of the finances. And why didn't he put Jiggs' name on the savings accounts?

He parked, changed into ditch digging clothes, and took the ham sandwich to Ox's house.

No one answered.

Opening the door, he went inside, stepping over boxes and piles of junk. It was messier than it had been last night. "We need to talk whether you want to or not," he called out. A quick check of the rooms showed no one was there.

Jiggs hurried for the ledger. Nothing on the desk had been moved. He turned pages, looking for expenses marked 'paid.' When the phone rang, he marked his place with his thumb and picked up the receiver. "Yeah?"

"Dad, what're you doin' there?"

"I'm doin' about thirty things at the same time. Why're you calling here?"

"Looking for Gramps. I called the bank, too, looking for you."

"What d'ya need? I'll be there to help as soon as I can."

"Well, it may take you a little longer. I got a call from Roscoe Zalman. He said Gramps drove him off the road again, but this time he was on the tractor."

"Oh...crap," Jiggs groaned. "Going where?"

"I figured home, but obviously he's not there. Maybe he's in town. This morning he told me he had to get groceries and to punch Old Man Tower in the gut."

"Crap. If he's losing his memory, why can't he forget *that*? I don't have time for this today. We've got to get the creek cleared. And now I'm wondering if the taxes have been paid. Did you borrow mules for this afternoon?"

"Not yet."

"What've you been doing? Why're you calling Ox?"

"Why're you getting bitchy? I'm the only one who's done any work today. I'm covered in sweat and sawdust, and I don't have any food or water."

"Well, whose fault is that?" He hung up.

Forget Ox. Jiggs walked out of the small house and tossed the sandwich into his Ford for Nap. He was at his own sink, filling the big orange thermos with ice water, when the phone rang again. It jangled ten times before it finally stopped. Good. He didn't have time for jabber or problems.

It began ringing again. Crap. "Hello!" he shouted into the receiver.

"Jiggs?" Bazz's voice carried a hint of urgency. "Ox is here in town."

"Go sabotage his tractor so he has to stay there. He's already chased one person off the road today."

"I took his keys from him. That was after he hooked the winch and chain to Old Man Tower's gate and pulled it out. It seems Tower wouldn't come out and talk with him."

"Oh geez. Where is he now?"

"He and Tower were taunting each other like cocks getting ready to fight. I thought about letting it go on. I could've sold tickets. Boy those two can really cuss."

"You should've let one of them knock the other down. Then it would have been over. I suppose you want me to come get him?"

"Go to Miz Cliva's. He walked off, saying he needed to talk to her."

146

If A Horse Doesn't Want To Go There...

THE DAMAGE AT Old Man Tower's place wasn't bad. Ox had pulled up a post; the gate had folded. Jiggs remembered the old door had dragged and only opened part way. The mess would be easy to fix, and it would work better than it had previously, but it was one more thing to add to his ever-growing list.

He parked in front of Miz Cliva's two-story, white clapboard house. An enamel kettle of red geraniums sat on the front porch. An American flag flew from a corner pillar. She'd been his teacher in the third grade and nice—for a Spinrad. She had a calm way with kids, listening to them and looking them in the eye without making them feel small. She probably had the same effect on old men. At least Jiggs hoped so.

Fat clouds inched eastward through a blue sky. The light wasn't playing tricks. For once, he wished it would. An extra hour or two would be handy today. He had more chores than minutes to do them. Two voices softly bumbled from inside the house. He pulled a bloom from a lilac bush and sat on the top porch step. He'd spare a minute to collect himself before confronting what was inside.

Inhaling the sweet floral scent reminded him of sitting on the patio with Ox, only a few days ago and wondering about a skull. He'd gladly go back and stop time there. Now he'd been sired by questionable ancestry. He'd soon have a lot of worthless land if he couldn't get water to it. Creditors may be knocking on his door any minute. And his father was...

What was wrong with his dad? That skull seemed to have set him off. Or maybe, as Little McGinty hinted, Ox had always been crazy.

The door opened, and Miz Cliva stepped out. "You're welcome to come in, you know. Would you like lemonade? I keep the cups in the freezer so they'll be frosty."

"No ma'am." Jiggs removed his hat. His dad stood behind her, carrying his hat in his hand, too. Years ago, Miz Cliva had made Jiggs write two hundred sentences: *I'll take off my hat indoors and when I talk to a lady*. She'd asked him to re-do the last fifty sloppy lines. "It looks like you really don't mean what you're promising." From that day, Miz Cliva's voice rolled around in his head if he didn't remove his hat when meeting a lady. He wondered what Ox's excuse was. He never had to deal with her in school. "Thanks ma'am. I'm the taxi service for your visitor."

"We had such a nice chat." The eighty-four-year-old grabbed Jiggs' arm, steadying herself as she came down the steps.

"I'm drivin' the tractor home," Ox groused, walking past both of them.

If Miz Cliva hadn't been hanging onto his arm, Jiggs would've commented how Ox had missed a few mailboxes on his way to town. Maybe he could wipe out the rest of them on the homeward trip. But if he popped off with the comment, he'd get stabbed with a Teacher Look: disapproving eyes and a frowning mouth. Instead, he only said, "There's been enough excitement for one day. We'll get the tractor later. Miz Cliva, thank you for the hospitality."

She didn't let go of him. She leaned her head close and whispered, "He's tired. Real tired."

"Of what?" Jiggs' said.

"Of more than you can ever imagine." She patted his hand and stopped walking, waving to Ox, who was already at the truck.

Ox tipped his hat. "Bye, Cliva. And thanks."

Now she gave Jiggs a different Teacher Look. The one they gave at graduation that said we're sending you out into the world. *Think before you open your mouth.*

Ox felt worn out as though he'd been hauling rocks. Cliva had convinced him to let the weight he was carrying drop. Now his muscles were limp. It felt like his bones were sinking to the bottom of his body. A weary relief. He wished he hadn't taken a swing at Tower earlier. "I need an aspirin or somethin'. My arm hurts." He waited in the truck while Jiggs hurried into Grubbs and sorted through the First Aid supplies they'd had since WWI.

The drive home was silent—for the first half mile.

"Dad...what're you doin? Taking off like that?"

Ox stared into his lap. Now of all days, his son wanted to gab. For the last thirty years it had been like riding with a rock. He considered ignoring him, but Jiggs would only talk louder and keep prodding him. "I needed to talk to Cliva. All I had was the tractor. Tried to talk to Tower too, but he said he couldn't come out—his gate was stuck. I unstuck it for him."

"I would've taken you tomorrow. What was so important?"

Ox thought a moment. There weren't words for it. Just an aching pull to get thoughts off his mind and the urgent feeling he shouldn't drag it out. "I felt like talkin' to somebody who knew your grandmother and your mother."

The truck rattled down the bumpy road, neither man speaking—for another half mile. "Why? You never talk about her. Who *was* my grandmother?"

Ox let out a long sigh. "It's water under the bridge. Damn people and their problems. Best done and forgot. Cliva says I should tell you. It'd be easier to carry around. And you'd stop bugging me." Jiggs didn't say anything.

"Your granny was Violet Spinrad." Ox glanced at his son. "You don't seem surprised."

"I'd already heard it. I guess if we have Spinrad blood, we must have a direct line to God."

"If so, it didn't do Violet any good. The diphtheria took her children, save one, Lowell. So your grandpa married her. I guess he still had some family dignity, a skosh of 'Albrecht' left in him at that time. Violet got pregnant.

"Lowell was hangin' around the barn when it was her time. That's what they did in those days, put the kids outta the house. He was only five and all by himself. It'd been rainin' hard for a week. Even all the way out there, he could hear his mama screamin' over the thunder and showers. All the night before, she'd been tryin' to have the baby. Albrecht came from the house and told Lowell his ma was in trouble and to ride to the neighbors and get Mrs. Byrd.

"He jumped on an old broomtail and rode it bareback. When he got to the creek, it was floodin' past the mare's withers. The nag rose up, and Lowell hung on, knowin' if a horse don't wanna go somewhere, then you can bet, you don't wanna go there either. Lowell beat that horse until it plunged in the water and swam across.

"It was chore time when he got to their farm, and Mr. Byrd wouldn't let his wife come until everything was done. Then he insisted they eat because there might not be time later. Only then did he hitch up the wagon and drive her over. He even stopped at the creek, waiting for it go down, but it didn't, so he finally crossed.

"To hear Lowell tell it, he was pleading and crying and beating on the man. You know the rule. You come when your neighbors call. They wouldn't ask if it wasn't important.

"By the time they got there, Violet was dead. That left Albrecht with Lowell and me. My mother died birthing me."

"Ohhh..."

Ox felt his son staring at him, but continued, "That's when it all went to hell—when I came along." He rubbed the ache in his arm. "Dad soon lost all of his 'Albrecht' and became 'Brick.' Mostly neighbor folk raised me until I was big enough to be weaned. Then Lowell watched over me. Brick took up with a floozy, Beulah Furling. She was a big, bony woman. Her face was long and her eyes wide like a giraffe's. That's what Lowell said. I never saw a giraffe or even a book with one in it back then. She thought Brick had money. Maybe he did, but it was gone by the time I got big enough to know what money was.

"She made beer. Had a still. That was Lowell's and my job—to watch the still. That's when Brick started drinking. We boys lived in the hen house 'cause she made our home into a saloon. She wore a big wide belt, and she used it on us if we sassed her. Dad would touch her arm, and speak in this sing-songy voice, 'Now Buelly, I don't think the boys mean any harm.' I don't know which was worse. Her beatings or him watching it with that spineless, wide-eyed look like he was gonna be next."

Ox glanced at his son again, relieved he wasn't asking any questions. The air in the truck felt sticky with misery. Finally he let out the breath he wasn't aware he'd been holding. "We had to leave before Lowell killed her. He swore he would."

"Good grief. How old were you?"

"Seven. He was twelve."

"Where'd you go?"

"Stayed in the woods. Helped on farms. There was enough work to get a meal most nights. Then the Great Depression came. Suddenly, everybody was poor. Homeless camps everywhere. I fought a grown man over an apple. An apple for hell's sake. Now, I see 'em, layin' by the side of the road, rotting. I think how we became animals tryin' to survive. I'm not proud of some of the crap we did, but we only got to eat ever' few days. Thank God for the war. Lowell signed up. I worked on a Kansas dairy, delivering milk. At least 'til I could lie and look old enough to get into the service."

"And after the war?"

Ox stared at his hands in his lap. He flexed his fingers open and closed. Only a few joints hurt. They'd never failed him through a lifetime of work.

"Lowell didn't make it," he said. "Died in the Philippines." He rolled down the window and closed his eyes, letting the breeze blow against his face. Jiggs had slowed down. That was all right. The truck didn't bump as hard over the road. "I rode that no-name mule all the way from Kansas. It was one of the best adventures I ever had. Dad was still alive. I couldn't believe it. Beulah wasn't handy using a whip on a grown man. She was only good at beating boys."

"So what did she do when you showed up?"

"All the land had been sold off. It didn't take much pressure to get her to look for richer pickings. She'd milked the place dry. Only the saloon-house was left, and I burned the whole damn place to the ground. I wished Lowell coulda been there to see it."

"What happened to Brick?"

Ox shook his head, staring out the side window. "I ask myself that a lot. How could I have come from a man who could watch me work until I staggered and fell into a bedroll every night? Then he'd sip booze and complain of aches until dawn. He was a damn, worthless drunk. I got back what he'd lost, though. Especially our name. I knocked heads with anybody who insulted a Woolsey."

He poked the air with his finger. "Nobody. I mean nobody made fun of you or your brother because of your grandaddy's drunk stupidness. I made sure you didn't have to grow up with the shame I did. Nobody was gonna call you dim-witted or a 'chip off the ol' Brick.'"

"You do," Jiggs said quietly. "You make a point to tell anyone who'll listen what a disappointment I am."

"That's different."

"Oh, that makes it all right?" A hard silence wrapped around them for several miles. Finally Jiggs said, "You never said what happened to Granddad. Where's he buried?"

Ox stared at the fence line passing by his window. He leaned against the door and let out a long breath. Cliva was wrong. Unburdening didn't make a damn thing better. It only led to more questions. "It's all past and blown over. I'm tuckered out," he sighed. "We can talk about it tonight. I'm tired of discussin' the sonuvabitch."

"I'll stop at the Bar and Grill and pick up a couple of meals. We'll talk over pot roast. How's that?"

"We'll talk after. I don't wanna ruin my dinner."

"So is that Albrecht's skull you stomped to pieces?"

Ox's world seemed to go white for a moment. He'd raised a son who had little respect for him. Maybe this was his fault. It was true, he hadn't coddled his boys, but he'd taught them what they needed to know. And he'd left them a legacy. Sure, he'd been a mean S.O.B. at times. He'd pulled underhanded things to survive. He'd even been accused of murder, but Jiggs had no idea of the battles he'd fought so the dumbass could enjoy the life he had. He just kept overstepping.

"Pull over for a minute." Ox waved a hand. "Here."

The Ford braked to a stop. "What is it? You look a kinda sick," Jiggs said.

Ox got out. He should backhand Jiggs and bust his lip, but it would take too much energy. All he wanted was to get away from his sorry shithead of a son. Slowly, putting one foot in front of the other, he headed toward home, confirming he was right. The road needed gravel. The county commissioners were probably embezzling again.

Behind him, Jiggs followed in the pickup. "Oh, c'mon, Dad. I'm sorry. Get in. C'mon."

It was satisfying to make him grovel. After forty feet, Ox paused and let the Ford pull alongside. Putting a hand on the open window, he leaned on the truck and rested.

"Dad, I'm sorry, but we don't have time for this today. I've gotta get over to Starvation Ridge. Please get in."

"I'm not riding with you. You're an ungrateful little shit. Your brother was never such a disappointment."

"Maybe if he'd lived long enough, he would've been as frustrating as me. But I'm all you've got. So we're stuck with each other. If I lower the tailgate, would you at least ride in back?"

Ox looked up the road then stiffly turned and looked behind him. No one was coming to the rescue. He nodded, hoping Jiggs wouldn't go fast and buck him out.

Beginning Is Easy, Continuing Is Hard

"YOU'RE LOOKING WASHED out. You want me to call a doctor?" Jiggs watched his father lie down on his bed.

"No. Dammit. Quit buggin' me. I didn't sleep good last night, and I haven't eaten all day. I'm tired."

"I've got a ham sandwich in the truck. I'll get it." Jiggs hurried out the door. When he returned, Ox was sleeping. His chest rising and falling, to the rhythm of a slight snore. Jiggs left him alone. After the day he'd had, he deserved some rest.

Jiggs stowed the sandwich in the fridge. As he left, he stepped into the alcove and took the checkbook. Outside, he jammed his truck into gear and sprayed gravel pulling out. He hadn't meant to, but half the day was gone, and he still hadn't done a lick of work.

He shouldn't have pushed about the skull. It seemed to be part of some play that had started long before he had gotten a role or a script. Once Ox had started talking, Jiggs wanted to get as much information as he could. His dad would probably clam up at dinner tonight as though his childhood had never happened. He'd suspected his dad's life had been dismal, but he hadn't guessed how bad. Tonight he'd listen and he'd keep his mouth shut.

Urgency kept picking at the edges of his thoughts. Getting water onto Starvation Creek had to be his first priority. Then he'd contact the folks they did business with and make sure they'd been paid. Somewhere in-between all this, he'd take the finances away from Ox. And what to do about the old truck? He couldn't lie that a part needed to be ordered forever.

Get the tractor popped into his mind and onto his to-do list. He and Nap would be burning gasoline like crazy, running around and fixing all the problems Ox had created. He pulled into Slat's Gas Station.

The owner gave a chin nod as he unscrewed the Ford's gas cap. "Hey, Slat." Jiggs watched him punch electronic buttons then load the nozzle into the gas line. "Sorry to trouble you, but we lost a few pieces of mail at the house. I wanted to check if our account's up to date."

The man lifted his ball cap and resettled it on his matted hair. "Boy, I'm glad you said something. I didn't want to mention it. I'll get you a total." He headed for the shop.

Jiggs watched the numbers click upward on the gas pump and wondered how many more checks he'd be writing.

Slat handed him the bill. "Did you ever figure out the owner of that watch you found?"

"Nope. It was smashed. Nothing to identif—"

BOOM! roared to the north. It rolled over pasture land and blew beyond the garage. Windows rattled in their frames as it passed. A single can of oil fell from the top of a pyramid-stacked pile.

"What the hell was that?" Slat looked up slack-jawed. "Sounded like an explosion."

Jiggs was already pulling the nozzle from his truck. He jammed it into the pump, yelling, "We'll settle up later." His tires screeched. He ignored Maxine Greenwald shaking a finger at him as he shot away from the station.

It was hard to tell the origin of the sound. Definitely to the northwest. He drove fast, fighting to keep the truck on the gravel road. It had to have been Nap. Who else would be blasting today?

The gate was closed as he wheeled into his property turnoff. He considered ramming it. He honked, though he wasn't quite sure why. Maybe to let Nap know help was on the way? He jumped out and fumbled with the chain and padlock. He shook his head to clear it. He was thinking like a panicked man.

He left the gate open as he drove through. A cardinal sin, but no cattle were nearby. Dirt flumed into a cloud as he stopped. No other vehicles were there.

Clear water splashed and rippled in the creek bed. The flow was only half the usual amount, but it was running. He should be glad, but he felt dread.

Jiggs shouted. No reply.

He climbed boulders, grabbing brush and limbs as he scrambled up the side of the ridge. He yelled at Nap as he went, hoping snakes would run from his racket.

There were boot prints and chunks of cut-up tree. The base of the stump was still in the creek, but part of it had been sawed away, allowing water through. The errant channel had been dammed and lined with rocks, forcing the flow into the stream bed. There were no holes, no dirt blown away from blasting.

"Son of a monkey." Jiggs breathed hard, bent over, his hands braced on his knees. If the explosion didn't come from here, where could it.... He took off running again, sliding and skidding down the hill.

He reached his pickup, pulling weed seed and branches out of his clothes as he threw open the door. Clouds of dirt trailed him as he headed for the road. Several cows had found the open gate. "Bound to happen!" He pounded the steering wheel, honking, scaring most them out of the way. Driving through, he padlocked the gate, leaving three cows standing on the road.

Round up the cattle. It went on his list, in front of: *Get gas. Get the tractor. Pay all bills*—if he only knew what they were.

He gunned the truck to George's house. Nap had probably done all he could without George's mules. Now he and the fat man had blown themselves up in one of his dynamite-laced sheds.

As he sped down the gravel drive, Jiggs could see there were no trucks at George's. He jabbed at the horn. The truck had honked more today than it had its entire life. Mules brayed, sassing the horn. He jumped out of the cab, shouting.

No answer.

He hurried onto the porch and stuck his head in the door. "Where is everybody?" The place was neat. No blood or bandages or cabinets left open. No signs of a crisis. If the sound had been an explosion, it hadn't come from any of the sources he knew about.

Jiggs stepped out onto the wide porch, the adrenalin draining from his body. Slowly he took off his shirt and shook out the leaves and bugs he'd collected while sliding through brush on his downhill run. He shucked his jeans, too, and sat on the steps in his underwear, examining the scrapes across his shins.

He was tired. Now he knew what Ox felt after gearing up to fight Old Man Tower. It was as though the air had fizzled out of him. And tonight when he'd catch up to Nap, he'd... . What would he do? It wasn't his kid's fault. What could he do to a young man who was the victim of a dad who always thought the worst was going to happen? He'd keep his mouth shut. That's what he'd do.

Jiggs emptied his boots and beat his clothes against a porch pillar. They were still itchy when he put them back on. He drove back toward Starvation Creek to round up the cattle. He smiled to himself. At least one thing went right today. The panic and letting-the-cows-out would fortunately go unnoticed.

That was before he saw the flashing red and blue lights at the gate.

Sol Meyers had blocked the road with his cruiser so the cows couldn't get past unless they jumped the ditch. He and the Angus stood near the gate, watching Jiggs drive up. "I've been looking for you," the sheriff called as soon as he got out. "Nap said you might be here. Then Maxine Greenwald reported you 'burning rubber' in this direction."

"Get to the point. What's happened?" Jiggs had stopped growing at six foot two, but Sol had continued to seven feet. Height and weight hadn't made any difference. They still competed and treated each other like they had in high school. "Was there an explosion?"

"Seems so. George called it in. He's taking Nap to the hospital right now."

"Ye gods and fishes, Sol! Why didn't you say so? What's the matter with you? How bad is it? Where are they now?" The cows gathered around the two men as though listening.

"In route to Joseph. George said there was blood. Nap was screaming in the background, but I think he was mostly terrified of George's driving. He kept yelling, 'You're gonna kill us,' and 'For mercy's sake, let me drive!'"

Jiggs pushed a cow's black muzzle away as it nosed his arm. He never treated them like pets, but a few of the breeder cows recognized him as the-thing-that-brought-the-feed-bucket. "Was Nap cussing?"

"Not that I heard. George was stuttering and Nap was pleading to drive himself."

"He's really hurt if he's not swearing." Jiggs turned to leave.

"Wait up. There's more," Sol called. "There's a fire at your place."

"What!" Jiggs took two steps back toward the sheriff. "Is that where they set off the dynamite? My place?"

"Musta been. I haven't been there. George told me to call you and get folks over to help Ox. Then Nap started screaming, 'Watch out! Watch out!' I think George hit something. I heard a *clunk*. Then Nap was saying, 'Oh God. Oh God.' I sent a unit from Joseph to intercept them."

"Craphouse crickets! Did they wreck?" Jiggs unlocked and opened the gate.

"Don't think so. I heard George. He was praying, then I drove into a 'no service' area." Sol waved his arms shooing the cattle back through.

"How bad's the fire?" Jiggs pushed an Angus out of his way to lock up.

Sol gave a tight-lipped headshake. "Don't know. What do you want to do? I'll help where I can."

"I'm going to the hospital. You check on Ox. You'll need to haul him outta there if it starts burning buildings."

Your Safety Gears...

NAP'S EYES BLINKED open.

"Hey pardner. How you feeling?" His father's face fuzzed in front of him.

The young man squinted. "You...haben't call me that long time."

"Look who's awake, George."

"Wherz George? I can't see 'im."

"Lay back, don't strain. You'll tear your stitches. George is on the other side of the curtain. He's your roommate."

"Shiiiiit. Are we all dead yet?"

"I'm sorry. I'm so sorry, Jiggs." George's bulk was confined to a bed with an oxygen mask strapped to his face. "I hope he's okay."

"He's resting." Jiggs glanced at his boy then moved a chair from the foot of the bed closer to George. "Start at the beginning and tell me what happened up to now," he said quietly. "I promise I won't interrupt or get upset. Do you have the air to do that?" George's cheeks jiggled as he nodded.

"I'm sorry." George's thick fingers clamped onto his bed sheet. "Nap came by the house. Said he needed to borrow a sandwich and the mules. Boy was he proud. You shoulda seen him. He got that creek runnin' all by himself. He was dirty as a lumberjack, but he was pleased."

Jiggs nodded intently, reminding himself to keep his mouth shut. Not to push. He'd get more information that way. He'd do it now with George. He'd do it tonight with Ox. It would all work out.

George pushed a pink bendy straw under his oxygen mask and took a sip of water. Then he hovered the thermos over his bed table as though unsure where to put it. Jiggs clenched back his impatience and watched George push magazines out of the way. The thermos finally found a spot to land. "Nap fixed a sandwich, one for me, too. Cleaned everything up when he was finished. He's a real polite boy. He may not do that at home, but he did it at my place. Anyway, we were sitting on the patio, eating and drinking lemonade, and I said, 'You can't handle Winston and Marlboro by yourself. It takes a man on each mule.'"

"He didn't believe me. In that way, he's like all young men, more spit than shine. I told him about takin' Marlboro and WildAss, my bull, to the back of my property. I tied 'em together and let 'em go. That bull snorted, pawed dirt, and lay down, but Marlboro stood there, his ears all laid back, bidin' his time. He kicked that bull when it got too close. Every time there was a little slack in the rope, Marlboro took a step toward home. That's the thing about mules. They always get home. By the time the pair walked into the corral the next day, that bull was broke. I could lead, load, and haul him anywhere. Marlboro, however, was pissed. He won't go near cattle anymore."

Jiggs took a breath and tried to let it out slowly and quietly. Finally he nodded toward the next bed. "Nap?"

"Oh yeah. Well, after hearing the mule story, Nap said he'd wait for you. Then we started talking about blowin' stumps with dynamite. And Nap said, 'I don't feel comfortable doing it on a hillside. Too many things could go wrong, besides it's

162

illegal.' And I had to agree. Smart boy you got there. We wouldn't want to lose our grazing rights on BLM land. So we decided to do a round for fun on flat ground. Just a little charge." He held his stubby fingers inches apart.

"And when Ox was here last night, he wanted to watch if we detonated anything. He'd be disappointed if we left him out. So we moved the whole shebang over to your place."

Jiggs felt George's gaze, but he didn't look up to meet it. He was quietly gripping the sides of the hard, round-bottomed chair, and keeping his mouth shut. He gave a go-on-I'm-listening nod.

"Ox thought it was a waste of dynamite to set it off like a firecracker. And I had to agree. It really would be a shame. So I showed Nap how to cut a window in that stump on the north edge of your pasture. I loaded the charge myself. I didn't let Nap do anything dangerous but light the fuse.

"That's all he had to do. Light the fuse and run. But he didn't run far enough. Ox and I were bellerin' at him, 'Run!' He started joggin' backwards. I guess he thought he might miss something if he turned and hightailed it. I was wavin' him to *C'mon.* He was shufflin' in reverse. Ox was yellin', 'Move, moron.' Then Nap tripped flat on his butt. He was tryin' to scramble up when the charge ignited.

"It was an old punky stump. Chunks and debris went sky high. I heard him whoop and cheer when it blew. It all woulda been fine except for that green-wood on the edge. His yellin' changed. 'Course we immediately drove my pickup out to him. He was big-eyed as an owl, starin' at a shard stickin' outta his leg. It wasn't the blast that hit him. It was the fallout. I'm so sorry. It shoulda never happened like that."

Jiggs waited for the story to continue. When it didn't, he prompted, "The trip here..."

"Oh! Then Ox told him, 'Don't just lay there and bleed.' He tied a bandana around Nap's leg, but Nap ripped it off. They had an argument about that. It was pretty heated, but we finally got Nap loaded into my pickup."

"And the fire?"

"Oh yeah. I thought Ox was going with us to the hospital, but way over at the fence line, up against the trees, smoke was curling from the ground. A charred piece musta landed there and flamed up. I dropped Ox at the barn. He said he'd take care of it.

"I drove as fast as I could. I'm not a good driver when I speed. Especially when I was tryin' to talk on the phone at the same time. I couldn't give Nap the phone, though he was tryin' to take it. I couldn't understand half of what he was yellin'. I got hold of the sheriff. I told him to find you and to call somebody to help Ox. I panicked. Ox is probably cussin' me about everybody comin' to see how two old codgers started a fire, but I didn't know what else to do. I was passin' and swervin around cars. I hit somethin'. It was big, but I kept goin'. I got your boy here to the hospital as quick as I could. He's gonna be okay, isn't he?"

Jiggs hesitated a moment, trying to keep his slow burn in check. "They're worried about infection, but they got the hunk of wood out of his thigh. They're watching him overnight. Thanks for getting him here. Are you gonna make it?"

"Yeah. Yeah. When I got here, I fainted in the parking lot. Good thing I didn't do it driving, huh? It was *some* trip, let me tell you. My blood pressure went through the roof. They wanna keep an eye on me, too. Did it burn much of your pasture? Is Ox mad?"

"Don't know yet. I don't carry a phone. I'll head home in a while to see. I'll stop at your place to feed the mules. Anything else you need? Want me to call your kids?"

"No. They won't come unless I'm dyin'. Look, I'm sorry. It shouldn't have turned out like this."

Jiggs stood. "That's why they call them accidents. They aren't supposed to happen. You work on getting your blood pressure down. Can I bring you anything?"

"A sandwich would be good."

"Now that you mention it, I could use one. I'll see what they have here."

Jiggs sat in the cafeteria with his eyes closed, rubbing his forehead. He should take George his sandwich, but he didn't want to go back. Not just yet. George was scared, but he didn't have the goodwill to comfort him. Not yet. George should've known better. And Ox? What was the matter with him? How many times had he ranted, "Your safety gears are between your ears?" Usually he'd add a few cusswords. Then he would rip a new hole in Jiggs for pulling a rattlebrained stunt.

And how many stupid things had he continued to do anyway?

"You want some company?"

He looked up to see Sol standing next to the table, hat in hand. Jiggs pushed a chair out with his foot. "Sit down. I was wondering how we lived this long with all the escapades we pulled."

"That's the Sixty-four Dollar question."

"How's my ranch?"

"You've still got a place to sleep. You look like you've been rode hard. You doing okay?"

"Better than George. He's scared. I don't know if he thinks I'm gonna throttle him, or that his heart's gonna explode, or that he ran over somebody on the way here."

"He hit a chicken. Actually it was a plywood cut-out of a chicken about yea-big." Sol held his hand over his head. "It was an advertisement for home-grown eggs. He clipped a few bushes, too."

Jiggs snorted a chuckle. "I shouldn't laugh. How's Ox?"

"It wasn't much of a fire. A few drifts of dead leaves piled against the fence from last fall. The grass was green. It didn't spread. Dooley Monroe got there before me."

"Sol. You're still in uniform. You haven't answered one of my questions directly. What's going on?"

"You're going to ask me to tell you this again. So I'm going to start at the beginning and tell you in the right order. Okay?" Jiggs stared at him as he continued. "Ox had saddled that big blue roan of his and used him to haul a bucket with wet gunny sacks to the burn. Dooley and I grabbed them and started whipping the fire."

"And Ox cussed you for doing it wrong. He's been touchier than usual."

"No. When the fire was out, he simply got on his horse. Without saying a word, he and the roan sauntered back toward the barn."

"Dad's not much for small talk."

"Jiggs." Sol leaned forward. "That horse made it about twenty feet. Ox hit the ground."

"What?" Jiggs straightened out of his slouch "He's never fallen off a horse. Ol' Blue wouldn't misstep."

"I used the AED unit in my car. I shocked him several times. There was never a pulse. He was gone before he fell off."

"Are you saying Ox is dead? He died fighting that fire?"

"No, it seems to me, now that I think about it, he was in pain during the fire. He watched Dooley and me put it out. When it was over, and the ranch was safe, he pulled himself onto his horse. That had to hurt like a son of a gun. What I'm telling you is that he died riding Ol' Blue. I'm sure that's the way Ox Woolsey wanted to go out."

Jiggs blinked. It felt like someone had trapped him under a jar. Everything was muffled. He should feel grief. He should feel something. He was sure Sol was saying something important. Words that were supposed to comfort.

Right now all he could think about was the talks he and his dad would never have. About doing something right as a son. About Brick. About family history. About the skull. About anything. Tonight or ever. He was leaving all the things he didn't want to deal with and riding Blue away from 'damn people and their problems.' *That* was the way Ox Woolsey *chose* to go out.

Someone was clasping his shoulder. "You still with me?"

"Tell me again, Sol. Slower this time."

"Three May Keep a Secret, If Two of Them Are Dead"

DEATH WAS ALWAYS an aloof old thief. He liked to sneak in, take what he wanted, and then make cruel demands on the survivors. They rarely had time to sort through their thoughts; instead, they were left holding a bag of goodbyes. Decisions flew at them from all sides.

Fortunately, Two Pan had participated in more than their share of funerals—as the census count would attest. Folks closed rank, even if they had no particular love for the deceased. Years of experience had established that Cleova Klegg would organize the death dinner. Lottie Lubach's macaroni casserole would be delivered to the family a week later. Spooner Hunter, the artist north of town, would write an obituary so glowing, nobody would recognize Ox. Some residents asked him to write their obits now, so they could roll around in their glory before they met their Judge.

The family was left with few tasks except selecting the venue: the Lutheran church, the Baptist church, or God's Hollow Cemetery. Most folks went with the Lutherans. Their coffee was free, and they threw in gelatin salads for the meals.

Everyone spread the announcement of the time and the date. And afterward, folks would say it was a nice service—even if Millie's dog had howled from the back row when the singing started.

The months that followed were the brain twisters. The numbness wore off just when it would've been handy to have it around to deal with wills, tax returns, and attorneys. Days ran together. What seemed like yesterday was actually a week ago.

Time got stuck, but as anyone in Two Pan could tell you, it would eventually jar loose. Regardless of who had exited the journey, morning kept breaking, tomorrow kept arriving, and folks continued to look for rockjacks of hope.

Jiggs stood on the porch of the two-story, white clapboard house. He scanned the view, comparing it to the last time he'd been here. The lilac blooms had dried and blown away. A tangle of red geraniums trailed out of their kettle. The flag still flapped from the corner pillar.

"You can come in, you know." Miz Cliva smiled from her doorway. "I've been expecting your visit."

He took off his hat as he entered and sat in the rocking chair that she waved him toward. "How have you been?" he called as she left for the kitchen. He looked around for a place to set his hat, finally resting it on the floor beside his chair.

"I'm fine, but let's skip all that and talk about what you really want to know." She carried a tray into the room and Jiggs stood, her etiquette lessons from third grade, poking his thoughts. "Please, sit. I expected you last week, so the brownies are a bit chewy, but the lemonade is cold." She set the treats in front of him and picked up his straw hat, placing it crown-side down on a side bureau.

White frost coated the mugs of lemonade. Jiggs took a gulp, unsure where to start. "So you expected me to drop by?"

"Yes, of course. I was one of the last people to see your father alive, and I told him to talk to you. I'm guessing he may have."

"Some." Jiggs nodded.

"How are you feeling about Ox being dead?" She gave him a Teacher Look as though she'd asked him to critique *Moby Dick*.

His forehead furrowed. "Honestly?"

"I'm guessing, you're going to ask what Ox and I talked about. We can speak around the subject, but if you want me to answer *you* sincerely, then you need to speak to *me* plainly and truthfully. Adult to adult."

"I'll try, though I still think of you as my third-grade teacher." Jiggs took a drink and then a big breath. "Honestly. I'm not sure how I feel about his passing. Mostly, it's a comfort, and then I feel guilty for being relieved. That's a sad thing, isn't it?"

"Not at all. He was a hard man to be around. Your mother talked a lot about him. You need to remember people express grief in different ways. No one is wrong. Your dad went through terrible mourning when your mom passed—though he wouldn't admit it."

"He was bitter. I never saw him break down."

"Heavens, no." She gave her head a tiny shake. "His way was to fix things. He knew grief was always sneaking around, but he did his best to fortify himself so it would have a devil of a time breaking in. There are no 'shoulds,' Jiggs. No rules on grieving."

"Maybe there ought to be. If he'd told me earlier about growing up hard and homeless, I would've been..." He fell silent, wondering if he would've acted differently.

"I've been through four wars." Miz Cliva concentrated on wrapping a paper napkin around the bottom of her sweating glass. She folded and creased each tuck as though it were important. "And then there was the Depression. We learned not to get attached to things. It was easier to bear when they were taken away. Ox practiced the lesson more than any of us."

"Did he tell you I found a skull?"

"I urged Ox to reveal its history. I thought you could carry some of his..." she looked at him, "...story. I'm glad you came to discuss it."

"He didn't tell me ma'am. We were supposed to talk that night but..." Jiggs looked out the window at a fern bush swaying in the wind.

"Do you still wish to know?" she asked. He nodded. "Then I shall tell you. But we'll need better comfort food."

She returned from the kitchen with a pitcher of lemonade and a tin of homemade chocolate chip cookies. She pulled her chair until it was directly across from Jiggs with only the span of the coffee table separating them.

"First, I must tell you that the older you get, the more secrets you collect because you've outlived the others who knew them. Someday, you'll understand what I mean. Ox told me you had found the skull. We decided he should tell you about it. You must know that it was hard for him. He'd lugged the guilt of those bones for over half of his life."

"There's more than a skull?"

"The whole body is buried there."

"Holy mooing cow." Jiggs' eyes widened as he leaned back, forgetting he was in a rocker. "Who?" he asked as he steadied himself.

Miz Cliva stared at her hands for a moment. Then she poured more lemonade, her face crinkling like leather as she frowned.

"I pieced together that it wasn't my great grandma," Jiggs said, filling the gap in the conversation. "As a reformed, two-dollar tramp, she's probably buried in a proper grave back in St. Louis. Great-Granddad is supposed to be resting in a plot in Flora. And I doubt if it was Ox's mother, Violet, who died giving birth. They wouldn't have put her in a streambed. Hey." He cocked one eyebrow higher than the other. "I understand we're related."

Miz Cliva raised her eyebrow to match Jiggs'. "Distantly. Very distantly. We had Violet interred in the Spinrad plot at Enterprise."

"That only leaves a choice between Albrecht, his ugly floozy, or a bunch of bank robbers and strangers." Jiggs watched to see if any suggestion got a response.

Miz Cliva closed her eyes. "Albrecht was a kind, gentle man, walking around as though a thundercloud resided over his head. Ox wanted to put him away, but your mother pleaded for him. She made Ox build a house for him, and Albrecht promised to stop drinking. He tried.

"It was Lisette, not your dad, who mostly dealt with him. She kept him fed, his clothes washed, and retrieved him each time he got out of the drunk cell. She could put up with a lot.

"He had a spate of sobriety and finally got a job at a hardware store in Minam. They gave him a little cot in back so Lisette didn't have to drive him back and forth. He kept the place neat and the shelves stocked. All of us thought he was doing so well."

Miz Cliva let out a long breath. Her mouth twisted into a deeper frown. She pulled a thick, yellow-paged album from beneath the coffee table and leafed through fragile pages. When Jiggs started to speak, she gave him a silencing look.

"And then he stole a pocket knife. A pen knife, really. Just a little thing. He said he was straightening them in the display case and realized he needed one. When the owner noticed it was missing and asked about it, Albrecht sheepishly pulled the knife from his pocket. He said he planned to pay for it when he got paid. The owner pressed charges. I'm sure Ox had something to do with that." She handed Jiggs a ragged-edged, one-inch news clipping.

He goggled at the four lines. "He hanged himself in jail?"

"Ox was so upset. I'm sure some of it was guilt for putting Albrecht there. Some of it was anger that his father couldn't take his punishment like a man."

"He hanged himself on his own belt?" Jiggs' voice grew louder. "Didn't they have policies to prevent suicide?"

"Topeka Butler was a wretched peace officer—worthless as bicycle pedals on a wheel chair. I never voted for him. He said he felt horrible about what happened."

"And he was still sheriff?"

"Yes, for years, but that's another story."

"So why bury Albrecht in a stream?"

"He didn't. Ox wouldn't plant Albrecht's body anywhere close to the land he'd parceled away." She tapped her bottom lip with her finger. "I think he's in the Lostine cemetery. I believe that's what Lisette told me years ago, though I've never looked."

"So the skull belongs to...?"

"I'm getting to that. You keep sidelining me with questions." She paused, her face smoothing into a Teacher Look with an eternal calmness that reached her eyes. "'There is a time for everything...a time to be silent and a time to speak.'"

Jiggs let out an audible sigh and refilled his lemonade.

"Your mother and I were good friends." Jiggs looked up, and she nodded. "When your mom needed a break from Albrecht, she used to ride over to Zinnia's place. She was my niece."

Jiggs smiled. "I remember Zinnia Roggs. She used to take care of Pax and me."

"She wasn't Roggs back then. Before you boys came along, she'd married a vicious man. Like all the Spinrad women, she was tiny with delicate skin and a bird-bone body. She got duped and found herself in-a-family-way by a hateful scalawag. One of his shoulders jutted higher than the other, and he

173

leaned like he might fall over. He didn't work, but maybe that was because of his club foot. When he thought no one was looking, he was most unpleasant. Even Grandpa Spinrad told Zinnia she didn't have to marry the skunk, which was quite a shocking concession for such a moral man. But she said she felt sorry for Cal Mosley and wanted her baby to have a name."

Jiggs took a cookie and nodded. "I think I remember Dad talking about him. Guy looked like a rat? Cut off the water flow, trying to get gold out of the creek?"

"That's him. One day, Zinnia was at your mom's house, visiting. The time got away from them. She knew Cal would be cussing-mad about his dinner being late. But when she got home, he never said a word. He watched her fix the meal. They ate, and he didn't say a thing. When she stepped out back to throw the dishwater on a rose bush, there was her cat hanging from the eave. He'd strung it up by the neck with fishing line. Dead! And then he said to Zinnia, quiet-like, 'Don't ever be late again.'"

Miz Cliva leaned forward, grabbing her knees for support. "It got worse after that. He didn't want Zinnia to go anywhere. Your mama and I didn't see her for a while. Finally, Lisette rode her horse through the pastures, so Cal wouldn't see her coming. Zinnia was sitting on the back porch step, crying. All she had on was a bra and a dish towel wrapped around her for panties. That barbarous devil had taken a knife to the few clothes she had, so she couldn't leave the place.

"Lisette brought her underclothes and a couple of work dresses. Zinnia wore them if Cal wasn't around, but when she'd hear his old Chevy coming down the road, she'd run to the outhouse, take off the clothes, and hide them in there. He never used the privy—preferred the woods like a wild animal.

"One day Zinnia wasn't fast enough getting to the outhouse. He saw her dressed, but he didn't beat her. She was big and round with the baby by then. Instead, he burned her clothes, knocked the privy apart, and sold it as firewood. What kind of sick so-n-so does that?"

"Why didn't she leave him?" Jiggs asked.

"Yes, why didn't she?" Miz Cliva's face twisted, each word becoming more exasperated. "Because Cal threatened to kill her, her baby, and anyone who took her in. Zinnia wouldn't put a family in that kind of danger. I told Topeka Butler—that sloth with a pointless badge. He did nothing! He said he couldn't arrest Mosley for being mean. He had to assault someone first. Animal and wife cruelty were nothing back then." She took a hard bite out of a cookie, and then fanned herself with the rest of it as she sat back in her chair.

Jiggs rubbed his forehead, pulling his eyebrows back into place. He could see where this was going and why Ox had stepped in.

"When it got to be Zinnia's time, we started riding over to check on her every day. Fortunately, Cal hadn't been there for a while. He often took off and showed up days later—which was a blessing. So on the night he drove in, Zinnia pushed us out the back door of their tiny shack and told us to leave quickly. But we didn't. We crouched in the dry creek, watching them through the window.

"He started in on my niece right away. *Why wasn't supper ready? What had she done today?* Zinnia began frying the hamburger hash we'd brought her. He cussed and threw a plate against the wall right over the stove. She jumped like she'd been shocked with a cattle prod. He laughed at that. Quick-like, she dumped the hash into a pie tin and slid it onto the table. Behind her back, she picked up the meat fork—as though that was going to keep him away. Your mama was mumbling under her breath, urging Zinnia to grab a butcher knife. It was like watching a horror movie.

"Finally, some Spinrad part of Zinnia woke up. She yelled, 'I'm about to have a child. I'll be busy. So you'd better get used to food not being on this table the moment you drive in!'

"He sat at the table for a moment, and then his arm shot out and punched her right in the stomach. Heaven help us, I'll never forget it. I put bruises on your mama's wrist to keep her from tearing into that shack. I thought I was going to yank her arm out of the socket, dragging her to her horse. I shook her to get her to hear me. 'Go get Ox. Tell him to bring his gun!'"

Jiggs scrubbed his hand through his hair, staring at the floor. "Now I see why Dad—"

"No, you don't see a thing. As I ran back toward the shack, I picked up the shovel leaning against a tree. Zinnia was holding her belly with one hand, but still clutched the meat fork behind her. Cal was yelling, 'Whatta you doin' over there?' She dropped the fork, white-eyed, and didn't move. He stood, knocking his chair over. 'You wanna try somethin'? Here I am.' He opened his arms wide and stuck out his chest, but only for a moment. Then he grabbed her neck.

"It was dark outside and your mama ran past me before I could get hold of her, so I followed toting my shovel. She crashed through that door, screaming, 'You bastard!'

"Cal was surprised only for a moment then lunged and grabbed Lisette by the neck, too. He couldn't do much with both hands full of women, so he started shaking them like rags. I hauled back to smash my shovel in his face and...*Boom!* Right before my eyes, a hole erupted in the back of his neck. I saw the broken shaft of his spine as his head flopped over. I can still see it." She gave a tiny shake as though knocking the image loose. "He thudded flat on the floor. Took both women down with him."

She took a breath before continuing. "Lisette was the first to get up. She shoved a pistol in my hands so she could pull

Zinnia to her feet. The barrel was still warm. I pushed it onto the cabinet with a, 'Where did you get this?'"

" 'Saddlebag. Ox insists I carry one when I ride.' She was looking at Cal as she said it. His head was cranked in an unnatural angle. 'It's to kill snakes. Unfortunately, he grabbed me before I got it raised. What with him shaking me around, I was afraid I'd hit Zinnia or you. So I jammed that Peacemaker in his throat and...'

" 'Grab that other leg.' We hardly recognized Zinnia's voice. She already had Cal by his dirty boot. 'I want him out of my house. Out of my life.'

" 'And do what with him? It was self-defense. We'll let the sheriff take care of it now,' Lisette told her.

"But Zinnia was having none of it. She kept repeating, 'That's not the way it works here, and you know it!' In fits and jerks she tugged Cal's body toward the door. She wouldn't let go. To get her calmed down, we helped drag him out back. He left a crimson trail across the floorboards. She growled at me. I barely understood what she was saying, 'Go back in, Cliva. Get the shovel.'

"Lisette spoke to her like she was calming a child, 'Settle down now. We won't go to jail for killing him.'

"The light from the back door shadowed part of Zinnia's face, but the half we could see looked like a crazed being. Her voice sounded deadly, as though she were threatening wolves if they came closer. 'So what if we go through a trial? Even if we're acquitted, tongues will wag every time we walk into a store, a restaurant, or church anywhere in this county—for the rest of our lives.' She pointed at me. 'You think the school board will let you continue teaching after your name has been connected with a murder?' She was right and I knew it.

" 'And you.' She pointed to Lisette. 'How do you think the Daughters of Two Pan will treat a killer? If you ever have kids, they'll have to fight, defending their mama—the gun woman.

And why should you shoulder any blame for my problem? Or for doing what the sheriff should've done a long time ago? I'm not giving Cal the chance to foul up any more lives.'

" 'Zinnia, I understand,' Lisette told her. 'You've lived in terror. You're angry. Let's wait until we're all thinking more clearly.'"

Miz Cliva stopped speaking. Jiggs looked up. The old woman was gazing out the window, after a while she said, "Poor little Zinnia. She'd always been so quiet and docile. I can't imagine the brutality she must have suffered to have changed her like that." Miz Cliva shook her head. "But it turned out Zinnia was the clearest thinker among us that night."

"For Every Time There Is a Season..."

—Ecclesiastes 3:1

MIZ CLIVA SPOKE slowly and quietly as though she were peeking from behind a tree, watching a wild animal. "Zinnia was on her knees in the sand, digging with her hands. When she finally spoke, her voice was merciless and sharp, 'This is where it stops. We tell people he beat me and lit out. He's nowhere to be seen. That's it. Nobody else is going to be bothered by him. Either help me or get out.' So...we buried Cal. The rocks on top were supposed to keep him there."

"Good grief." Jiggs rubbed his hand over his chin and mouth. "I can't believe this."

"Zinnia was having hard cramps by then and we convinced her she needed a doctor. Lisette and I promised we'd come back later and clean up. We would've promised anything to get her into the only vehicle around—Cal's truck.

"We left our horses tied out back. By the time we got to Lisette's house, Zinnia was sweating and yelling. Lisette told Ox the blood on our clothes was from hemorrhaging. It was actually Cal's, but men don't ask questions about women's blood. Ox took off for the barn like all men do when intimate female issues transpire.

"Back then, we didn't have the hospital in Joseph. We waited for Doc Latham. There was screaming, hot water boiling, and the usual hand wringing going on." Miz Cliva gave Jiggs a frustrating stare. "But your father..." She shook her head. "Ox had such a tiring code of how things *should* be. While he was hanging around the barn, he noticed Lisette's horse wasn't there. He hooked up the trailer, picked up a crow bar, and drove to the Mosely place to have a man-to-man talk if Cal was still around.

"Right away, he could tell something was amiss. We had hurried out of there, leaving the light on and doors wide open. When he looked in the back, he couldn't miss the red trail across the dirt or the row of stones piled in the dried-up pool. The bloody shack told its own story, along with Lisette's gun on the cabinet where I'd forgotten I'd laid it. He checked her pistol, and found a bullet missing. Our secret went from three people to four.

"Ox turned off the light and closed the doors. He was on the porch when a truck drove up. Who would've thought the laziest lawman in the county would get in his car and drive over after the doctor had called? Doc Latham was raging when he saw Zinnia bruised, strangled, and miscarrying. He demanded that her husband be arrested immediately.

"So when Topeka Butler's headlights flashed across the Mosely shack, Ox was standing there with a gun, staring at him. As soon as the sheriff got out of the car, Ox confessed, 'I shot Cal Mosely for stealing cattle.' I suppose it was half true. Cal had rustled most of the ranchers in the valley. It was one of his few talents, and no one could catch him at it.

"Butler being a brilliant lawman, said, 'That's the best news I've had in a year. Where is he?'

"Ox looked around. 'Restin' out back.'

"From the look on Butler's face, the blood revealed Cal was resting a little more eternally than he had expected. The sheriff had this gesture he always did when he was thinking. He lifted his Stetson, smoothed his hair as though he was massaging his brain. Then he resettled his hat and did exactly what Zinnia had predicted. Nothing.

"Maybe it was because Butler hated Cal. Or he thought he owed a debt to Ox because he'd let Albrecht hang himself. Frankly, I think it was because Butler didn't want to do the paperwork. Whatever his reasons, he said, 'The way I see it, you've performed a public service. So I'm gonna tell you what happened here. The coward beat the baby out of his wife and took off. The county can't afford safaris in search of derelict murderers. If he ever shows up, I'll arrest him.'

"The sheriff's investigation concluded with burning down the Mosley shack because it was a 'fire hazard.' He and Ox unleashed the water Cal had pent up. It covered the stones and put a current back in Starvation Creek. That was about as much work as I'd ever seen Topeka do in his whole life. Zinnia was right. That was as far as justice went. Whichever path we chose, Cal would be dead. We could make a fuss out of it, but we'd only be blackballing ourselves and our families."

"But..." Jiggs squinted.

"It was 1957. Things were different then. The only forensic piece of equipment Butler had was a gun and an undeserved badge. Zinnia stayed out in the country with your family. She later told me that Butler declared Cal Mosley 'Missing—unknown whereabouts' in case anyone asked. No one ever has but you." She gave him a sad smile.

Jiggs looked out the window to see if the light had hung up. How could it be a normal day? The wave of the last fifty years was crashing over his head. "Last week I thought my family was upstanding members of this community. Now you're telling me Ox took the blame for murder to protect Mom? No. I'm not buying it. He wouldn't throw away everything he'd built up."

"If Butler had known that it was a woman who'd shot Cal, he wouldn't have reacted the same way. Lisette would've been arrested. Eventually, she'd have been acquitted. But at what cost? Ox didn't take the chance. He shouldered the responsibility."

"Why wouldn't he tell me all this?"

"And what would he say? 'Your mom killed a man.' Is that something you'd tell Nap about his mother if you didn't have to? Besides, it wasn't Ox's secret alone."

"But it was years ago. Surely by now..."

"After keeping a sin buried for so long, it becomes a habit. It's not natural to air it out and let it flap for everyone to see like dirty laundry. You have no idea what it's like in this town to carry a name that is trailed by whispers, but Ox knew. He made sure you didn't pay for the sins of his fathers—or your mother." Miz Cliva folded her hands in her lap and nodded with a frown, urging Jiggs to comprehend.

Silence settled in the room. Even the birds outside seemed to quieten. Jiggs rubbed his head, his hand stopping and holding the back of his neck. An ice cube in a glass made a *tink-tink* sound as it fell into a new position.

After a while, she spoke so softly it was almost a whisper. "Children only know part of their parents' lives and very little about the quicksand they've waded through. You seem to think this skull affair is all about you, Jiggs. I urged Ox to trust you and tell you. Your father took on Lisette's burden. Actually, four of us are indebted to him. He bought the land and made sure our secret stayed kept. And then you dug up the skull.

"I'm the only one left now. You have a choice: You may keep the conspiracy your father carried or you may reveal it to the community. It's up to you. But either way, you're one of the secret keepers of Two Pan now. Most of the old-timers are freighted with knowing the sins of others."

"But I'm still young. I'm only forty-five."

"Then you'll have a long time to hear your neighbors' stories and help carry their burdens. We never asked for this job. As I said, we've simply outlived the others." She held up the tin. "You look a little peaked. Have a chocolate chip cookie, dear. Take several. They're good for your heart."

They talked two more hours until the doves cooed from the hackberry tree, heralding the start of the afternoon. Miz Cliva bagged a few cookies to send to Nap. As they stepped onto the porch, Jiggs looked up and down the street. "Does everyone in Two Pan have skeletons in their closets?"

A corner of her mouth twitched. She looked at the sky with a private smile. "We only warehouse secrets, Jiggs. We don't distribute them." She pushed the cookies into his hands. "You look tired. Go home. Rest. 'To everything there is a season...' and grief about your father takes—as long as it takes."

He nodded and let out a breath. "Then there's one more thing I need to do."

"The Past is a Regret, The Future an Experiment"

—Mark Twain

JIGGS FLEXED HIS shoulders and leaned backward, his hand bracing the small of his back. He stretched as he watched Nap's quarter horse trot toward him.

"The message you left on my phone," his son called out, "'Meet me in the northeast corner of the ranch,' sounds like a challenge to fight after school."

"You came anyway."

"Figured I could take you."

"You wish. Get down here and run this pickaxe."

"What're we doin'?" Nap slid off the saddle and tied Face Punch to the fence post next to Curly Dogs.

"Prying a hole out of the ground." Jiggs held out the tool.

"I can see that. Why?"

"For your granddad."

Nap swung the axe, using the mattock side, chopping a chunk out of the clay. "Are we gonna dig him up and move him to this hole?"

"Just his secrets."

"I've been thinking about Gramps. I sat in his house the other day. It still smells like him. Sometimes he was funny, but

I don't know what to think about some of the stunts he pulled. He could be a royal pain."

"The old man you knew wasn't who he always was. That's what he aged into."

Half-closing one eye, Nap looked at his father, taking inventory for a long moment. "You're starting kinda early. Seems like after a person dies, people forget the crap they pulled. The deceased becomes a saint. If you're gonna tell me Gramps was a great guy and all those years of faultfinding were some kind of tough love, I'm not buyin' it yet."

"That's not what I'm saying. Keep going." Jiggs circled his hand. "Make the hole a little longer and deeper." He went to his saddle and untied a burlap bundle.

Starvation Creek hadn't been hard to block off. The pieces of skull had been easy to dig up. Under the large flat rocks, he'd found the long bones, including the calcified remains of a twisted foot. He had released the water again, watching it wash over Cal's empty resting place and carry the memory of him downstream.

"I'm saying..." Jiggs toted the bag to the digging, "that Ox kept his history close to his vest and spewed his opinions all over us. That doesn't change, but I've finally pried the secrets out of his life, and I'm telling you, he was more than the man we knew."

"How so?"

"That should be deep enough." Jiggs kneeled, untied the bundle, and placed the contents into the hole.

"Are those human bones?" Nap stared.

"They're from a man named Cal Mosely. To do this right, I suppose I should say something over him." Jiggs stood, studying the bones. "So, Cal, here's how you ended up like this. Your neighbors were Ox and Lisette Woolsey. Dad was a hard man who protected his family. Mom was a strong woman who righted a wrong."

185

He scooped up a shovelful of dirt. As he told Cal's story, he filled the grave. When he'd finished, he slapped the shovel against the clods, shaping them into a mound.

"I can't believe it." Nap helped him stack rocks on top. "I never would've suspected Gramps of that kind of concern. I knew he was angrier than usual before he died, but I thought it was old age, not because you'd dug this up. So why aren't you turning the bones in like you'd planned?"

"It took a while to get it through my hard head, but I understand why your granddad was right. He was protecting his family."

"I would've left this guy in the creek."

Jiggs gave him a quiet look. "Everybody deserves a decent burial, especially the family's skeletons."

Nap slapped the dust off his hands. "Is Miz Cliva relieved you're keeping the secret?"

"She simply shrugged and said, 'Do what you think is best. I don't feel guilty. Some men need killing.' All of this would've been easier if Ox had trusted me enough to tell me about his past. At least it might've helped me see why he was so hard. Why he did things the way he did. Why he grew into treating folks rough."

"But that's not who he was; and it didn't happened that way."

"Nope. He didn't talk to me—or most anyone else." Jiggs stared at the clouds, their ragged pink edges wisping away as they moved to the east. "With the history he was towing, I suppose he was doing the best he could."

"I wish we'd had more time to work that out."

"Yep." Jiggs glanced at his son. He wanted to tell him that death cut short a lot of conversations. That by the time a person had gathered enough sense to ask the right questions, the guide was usually gone. Life was mingy that way, making a person scratch for his own answers. But Nap wouldn't understand—not yet. It was one of those hard-knock lessons. "I suspect our opinions of Ox will change as we run into our own problems and see how we measure up. For now, we know him by what he left behind."

"The Rockin' W?"

"Yeah, but I meant he left his thumbprint on two good men."

"I suppose so. What do the good Woolsey men do now that we've buried the family skeletons?"

"I believe we let go of the problems we can't change." Jiggs gripped his son's shoulder. "That means you should try not to make the same mistakes as your father." His eyes cut away to the horizon. He gave Nap's shoulder a squeeze followed with two solid pats before letting go.

To the north, the hum of an airplane carried across the miles. They stared until it disappeared over Idaho. Jiggs shifted and tapped his shovel on the rocks. "Well, rest in peace, Cal. Your neighbors won't bother you anymore."

They tied the tools onto their saddles and mounted without speaking. To the south, the Eagle Caps watched over them. To the west, the light glowed in a sepia hue as it angled across the acres of Ox's legacy. "I'm guessing we'll have more time tonight." Jiggs checked the light. "Enough to catch a baseball after chores."

"Maybe Harriet will be the backstop, she likes to chase things. Are you gonna get rid of her, now?"

A smile played across Jiggs' face as he looked at his son—his legacy. "No. I figure Ox was right. Every ranch needs a quirky cow that makes you laugh."

"Today she was mooing at a squirrel that was throwing acorns at her. I had no idea dairy cows were so goofy."

Jiggs laughed. "Well, here's something else you didn't know...your great-great-granddad was fifteen when he left home to avoid the German army..."

The horses plodded to the beat of the story. Jiggs spoke of Bruno; then of Albrecht; and finally of the miners, madams, and misfits in the Woolsey family.

He and Nap would converse through the night. And in the wee hours of the morning, they'd still be talking of ear chips, robot cows—and the future.

Mornings break clear and cool in the far corner of eastern Oregon. The sun crosses the sky, shining on a girl riding a brown mare, her hair flying straight in the wind. A boy on a blue roan almost catches up to her laughter. The sun passes a house with a maple tree. Crows sit among the leaves, commenting on the forts two young boys are building in the hay. By evening, it travels over the pines. Below them, tilted headstones rest in the shade. Above, a breeze sighs through the branches.

The slanted light turns dusky and golden. Birds still themselves on their night roosts. Screen doors bang shut for supper. Time hesitates for a moment with the promise that there is still something left to the day. Gentle counsel to hold on, that all is changing. Then the sun slips to the other side of the world.

It's what makes the folks of Two Pan a little creative, a little eccentric, and a little sleepless—into the night.

***

Jottings

"Where is Two Pan?" Readers familiar with eastern Oregon ask. Their faces have that sincere look used for confessions and hospital conversations. "Really…" they nod. "You can tell me."

Okay. Sure. Mention Oregon and most folks picture green mountain forests sweeping west into the Pacific Ocean. A wide strip of the state is full of tourists, waterfalls, open-air markets, and coffee shops.

The other two-thirds of the country is the "dry side." The land of few people and even fewer roads. Black nights, bright stars, and crisp, mountain breezes make people lose their urban veneers and examine the cracks in their souls. There's something about eastern Oregon.

Folks familiar with the country have their favorite, secret spots. They'll be glad I didn't draw maps and give directions, so everyone could check them out. Instead, I shared my favorite place. A fizzled-out gold town with cows, cranks, and plentiful homespun advice. Folks generally tell it like it is, and if that doesn't work—nature herself has a way of pushing the living toward what they don't want to face.

Where is this speck of sage, spotty cell phone service, and miles between gas stations?

Well, it's sort of secret, but you can get there if you start at page one.

Welcome to Two Pan.

The development, design, and editing of this book would not be possible without: C. Walter, Ernest Knorring, William Vause. and E.T. Place This book was escorted into print with the insight and patience of Ken, David, and Greg. Thanks.

Hats off to the guys at the parts store, the cow-tail store, and the mercantile. (You know who you are—and I only believe half of the lies you've told me.)

B.K. Froman lives in an eye-blink of a town in Oregon with 14 moles and 34 mounds of dirt in the yard.

More humorous stories about change can be found at:

Before Morning Breaks
www.barbfroman.wordpress.com

Sign up for the NEWSLETTER to hear about new books and Two Pan News.

www.barbarakayfroman.com

Books in the Series...

Book 1: Mornings in Two Pan
Book 2: The Lights of Two Pan
Book 3: Women and Thieves of Two Pan

And now...

The Lights of Two Pan

Someone in Two Pan is awake tonight, just like you. Maybe you're standing at the grocery store reading this rather than some rag on how to lose twenty pounds in two weeks. Hopefully, you're lazing in a hammock while the moon rests on long rollers of a warm water ocean. Perhaps you're sitting in a doniker in the Rockies as a single star blazes to its end. God forbid you're trying to rest in some uncomfortable chair or hospital bed waiting—afraid to hope.

Wherever you are, it doesn't matter. Day or night. Or a continent away. Someone in Two Pan is awake with you right now.

It's not a city like New York that never sleeps. It's just that someone in Two Pan isn't sleeping.

In daylight, it's easy to see the residents juggling the uneven pieces of their lives, but come evening, you'd best look for a bit of light to see their struggles. A bare bulb hanging from a tree limb over an open truck hood. The lamp of a bedside vigil, outlining a window. A lantern casting half-shadows across faces in an open field.

In cities, neon bulbs buzz and hum without human company. In Two Pan, a lone point of light means a citizen is making a community improvement, working on her dream, or trying to keep the pieces of his life from crumbling apart.

These are forthright folks. You want an honest opinion, you'll get one. They'll tell you if a casserole needs more seasoning, if you shouldn't have tipped for your last haircut, or if your nephew is truly dumb and ugly. If you're gullible, they may embellish their advice a bit, but that comes from living in this unyielding land for so long. Sandwiched between granite mountains and tall sky, they've had to create their own diversions.

To find this hidden place, follow Highway 82, a skinny black line on an Eastern Oregon map. Two Pan nestles where it changes into gray patchy asphalt. From there a gut-jostling track takes you into the Eagle Cap Mountains. This little-known path of locals and savvy outdoorsmen winds through the gold camps of yesteryear. Once-exciting places such as Shiny Creek, Lilyville, and French Camp are now trailheads for the semi-daring. Little remains of the gold, in case you were thinking of quitting your job and taking up prospecting.

Local stories are not about the miners, but the folks who stayed to work and prod the land. There must be something in that beggarly soil, because fifth generation settlers still own many of the ranches. And therein lies the great mystery of Two Pan: Why are these folks so creative at resisting the shift and shuffle of change?

It's what makes them stubborn, eccentric, and sometimes—a little sleepless.

***

Come visit the folks of Two Pan.

Ebooks and Paperbacks are available through major on-line retailers...or...support your local bookstore and ask to order the Two Pan series.

Thanks for reading!

www.ingramcontent.com/pod-product-compliance
Lightning Source LLC
Chambersburg PA
CBHW032135170626
46808CB00006B/2239